# ALENA'S REVENGE

## K.A KNIGHT

Copyright © 2021 by K.A Knight

All rights reserved.

No part of this book may be reproduced in any form or by any electronic or mechanical means, including information storage and retrieval systems, without written permission from the author, except for the use of brief quotations in a book review.

Edited by Jess from Elemental Editing and Proofreading.
Formatted by The Nutty Formatter
Cover by Talk Nerdy 2 Me.

❦ Created with Vellum

TRIGGER WARNINGS

**This is a dark story. It contains scenes of torture and assault, knife play, blood play, murder, and other adult material that some may find triggering.**

# NOTE

**This story is not for the faint of heart. There are no heroes here, only villains seeking their revenge.**

## CHAPTER ONE

### Alena

F uck Travis. Fuck him and his stupid 'this isn't working anymore' shit. He was just scared we were moving too fast. Not that I had been all for it, but it was just working out that way since we spent most of our nights together at his fancy apartment. I tried to keep my distance, to go slow, but he was adamant about pushing ahead. He told me he loved me and had never met anyone like me before.

All fucking lies, lies he's probably telling some poor other girl right now.

He lives for the chase, the sex, and then breaking hearts. I saw the malicious grin on his face when I turned away, refusing to beg or cry. I deserved better, but that didn't mean it was painless. I loved him a little. It was fresh and still growing, but it was there, and now here I am, slightly drunk and wearing a ridiculously short dress and overly high heels. Why do I do this?

Why am I out here making a fool of myself just because some idiot hurt me?

I know better, he's not the first man to let me down, nor will he be the last, but I'm fucking tired of these boys and their games and the boredom in the normalcy of living. Work, sleep, heartbreak, repeat. So instead of my usual ritual of drinking myself into a coma at home, here I am, looking for something to change my world.

I guess I should be careful what I wish for.

When I see him, I know he's going to be my fun tonight, a faceless fling to rid myself of the feel of the man who couldn't even make me come. He's dressed in a suit and good-looking. Just what I need. Something in me screams in warning, but I toss back my shot and ignore my brain. After all, it's only led me into bad decisions and the beds of toxic assholes. For once, I won't be smart. I'll be stupid and take what I want.

Right now, that's him.

Grabbing another shot for confidence, I drink it down before straightening my shoulders, flipping my hair back, cocking out my hip, and heading his way. He's standing near the VIP section talking to a bouncer, and he finishes the conversation just as I sidle up to his side.

He blinks in surprise, but a slow, sultry smile curves his lips. "Well, hello there, beautiful. Looking for someone?"

"Yes, you." I grin, stepping closer, sliding my hand up his chest to tickle the bare skin exposed at the top. "You look like a good time, which is exactly what I want."

"Is that right?" he purrs, grasping my hips and pulling me closer. I hook my leg around his, and he inhales, eyes darkening.

"Yes, so are you?"

"Am I what?" he murmurs, his head bent towards me.

"A good time?"

"Definitely. Why don't you let me show you?" he offers.

I nod and he takes my hand, leading me up the VIP stairs to a booth at the back. He slides in and pulls me after him. I lose my balance and almost land on his lap, making us both laugh.

He strokes my exposed skin, running his eyes over my body. "What's your name?"

"Alena," I answer and lean closer, pressing my breasts against his arm, making him groan. "Yours?"

"Whatever you want it to be," he teases, his eyes dark. "Won't your friends miss you?"

"I'm here alone," I reply, and he blinks at my response, but it seems to be the right answer when he leans in and kisses me. I kiss him back. He tastes of whiskey and mint, and it's not unpleasant. When he pulls away, panting, I lick my lips.

"What sort of fun are you after?" he questions.

"The kind that has me screaming with my nails in your back," I purr, dragging my hand down his torso to his hard cock. I squeeze it through his trousers so he knows exactly what I desire.

"I do like a woman who knows what she wants." He grins and brushes his lips against my ear, making me shiver. "And isn't afraid to take it." He drops his hand to my long legs and runs his fingers up the smooth skin before reaching the hem of my dress. My breathing stutters, and my veins hum with desire and alcohol, but when I pull back, his eyes look... wrong. For a moment, I see a flash of satisfaction and calculation that makes me look closer, but then it's gone and he's back to smiling at me.

"Another drink?" he queries.

I nod mutely, internally shaking my head at my absurdity. It's the lights, smoke, and booze playing tricks on me. He waves his hand, and another drink appears before me—a fruity cocktail. I prefer straight vodka or beer, but I let it slide. He doesn't need to know me to fuck me. In fact, it's probably better that way.

"Bottoms up." He nods, sipping his drink as he keeps his eyes on me above the rim. I toss mine back, almost gagging at the excessively sweet drink. He drains his as well, taking my glass and adding it to his on the table.

"Want to come to my office for a little privacy?" he growls, dragging his fingers along my shoulder and playing with the strap of my dress. My pussy flutters a little at the invitation, and despite the alarm bells ringing in my head, I nod and let him take my hand and lead me from the VIP area.

Guiding me to a staircase, he rushes up the steps. I don't complain, happy to get down to business. The lights flash brightly, obscuring my vision, and my head swims slightly, probably from all the alcohol. Fuck. I stumble, but he chuckles and rights me. He yanks me roughly after him, and I fall into the closed door at the top, gasping as the breath is knocked out of me. He groans and slams my back against it, his mouth descending on mine again. I blink as he devours me. Everything is slowing down, spinning. He pulls away, and the next thing I know, I'm on a desk with him on top of me. I giggle automatically as he shoves my dress up, but I can't feel his touch. I feel numb.

Something is wrong.

The alarm bells are screeching now as my head spins. I want to close my eyes as my body becomes limp and unresponsive. My words even come out slurred. What's wrong with me? Surely it can't just be the booze, I didn't have that much.

"Fuck, you're sexy," he growls against my skin, nipping at it.

"Stop, something… something's wrong." I push at him weakly, barely even able to move him from between my legs.

"Too much to drink?" He laughs, but when he lifts his head, his smile is cruel. I blink. He has two heads now.

*Get the fuck out.*

I know if I don't get out of this room, something really bad is going to happen.

*Move now.*

I try to sit up, but he pushes me back. "No, no, what was in that drink?" I try to snarl, but it comes out as a gasp. My head spins and my eyes start to close. Everything begins to fade, and at the last moment, I throw myself away from him, but when I hit the floor and it all goes black, I know I'm too late. Especially when I hear him standing above me.

"Thought I would at least get to have my fun this time."

*Fuck.*

---

I REGAIN CONSCIOUSNESS SLOWLY. MY HEAD IS FUZZY, AND IT'S banging like a two-day bender headache. My body feels sluggish, and my skin is dirty, gritty, like I'm covered in sweat. Groaning, I try to pry my eyes open, but they refuse, and then I'm suddenly back in the black, and the pain stops.

Next time, I force my eyes open, and I squint at the dark room before I pass out again. My body is obviously still fighting off whatever is running through my system... whatever that asshole put in my drink.

Drugged.

I was drugged, I realise, before I succumb to the effects again.

I know time has passed when I wake up once more. I'm lying on something soft. I'm still weak and tired, but not as bad as before. The pain in my head has lessened, but I still don't feel a hundred percent. My nose twitches as I smell dampness, sweat, and even pee. Cracking open my eyes, I find my head lolling on what looks like a dirty mattress on the floor of a half empty room. There's a broken bed, old boxes, and furniture to one side. Dirty, ripped curtains cover the single window, where sun is trying to shine through the dusty, fogged glass.

Where am I?

I know something bad has happened. I was drugged, and now I wake up here? I move my feet and realise they are bare—no shoes, no bag.

*Get moving, Alena, this is not fucking happening to you.*

I see the news and hear the stories, and I refuse to be one of those girls on the reports.

No fucking way. I try to sit up, gritting my teeth against the pain it causes, but I just flop back down.

Time passes slowly, but each hour that slips by brings more strength into my limbs, and finally, I can stand. I manage to stumble around the room, inspecting the space. I try the window, but it's bolted closed and looks out over water. The door is also locked, and I try to pick it with a nail from the floor, but it does nothing. Exhausted and thirsty, I collapse back onto the mattress, telling myself I'll rest for a bit before getting out.

The next thing I know, there's a giant bang as the door opens, and then I hear the sound of boots stomping across the creaky wood floor.

"Wake up, cunt. It's time to make you pretty for your buyer." Someone kicks my floppy legs. "Get your ass up. You won't like it if I have to make you. It's time for your new life, whore." He laughs, the sound low and hateful.

Looking up in fear, I meet the eyes of the stern, smirking man.

Buyer?

Oh, double fuck.

---

### Idris

"It's done," I snarl, tossing the heads of the men I was sent to kill at Donald's feet. He runs his eyes over them and then me, noting the blood covering my frame—theirs, not mine. It was supposed to be an impossible mission, a mission for my freedom. He should have known better. No one can kill me, and when I set my mind to something?

I'm unstoppable.

Unkillable.

The fucking boogeyman in the shadows.

I'm the best he and the Clergy have. I've already been to see them to prove I survived. They thought it would kill me, they all did.

When I first approached Donald about my freedom, about wanting to retire, he thought I was joking. Everyone did. I understand why. I'm the best and I love my job, but I'm missing something in my life. I'm no longer happy. It's too easy, too empty. I need to be free of this and them. He promised nothing but took my request to the Clergy—the top of our business, the ones who control us. They clearly thought giving me a suicide mission would make me change my mind, would make me stay. After all, it's hard to find a cleaner, a boogeyman who will kill anyone they want.

Including their own.

I'm the fucking monster they need to survive, and they didn't want to let me go without a fight, but they forgot who they made, and I completed the mission, even if it nearly killed me, and now they have no choice but to let me go.

"They'll take it out on you," I warn, feeling a slight pang of regret as I stare at Donald. I wouldn't call him a friend, I have none of those, but we have been through a lot together.

"I know." He grins, uncaring. "They can try, but they need me, Boogeyman." He nods. "Are you sure about this? What will you do? Men like us aren't meant for a normal, civilised life."

"That's for me to find out," I grumble, stepping towards the door. "It's done, so I'm free?" I have to ask.

"We won't hunt you. You're free. Everyone else will think you are dead. We'll say it happened on your last mission. There is no returning, so lie low. If an agent sees you, there is no way we can defend this decision. Do you understand?" he questions, his shrewd eyes locked on me.

"I understand," I mutter, clenching my scarred, tattooed hands at my sides, feeling the dried blood on them. I didn't bother to shower, but I will when I leave here, even though my skin will never be clean of the blood I've spilled. My soul will never be anything but pitch-black from the deaths I've dealt in my life.

"Boogeyman," Donald calls as I turn. I freeze and he sighs. "Good luck, I mean it. I hope you find whatever you're looking for."

*As do I.*

---

Idris

*Five Months Later...*

A KNOCK SOUNDS ON THE DOOR OF THE COSY COTTAGE I CALL HOME these days, pulling me from my task of ripping out the cabinets in the kitchen. Frowning, I grab my shirt and wipe my face, ducking under the low beams as I open the front door.

"Oh," comes a feminine gasp. I look up with a frown, spotting Bessie there, her face coloured red as her eyes catch on my huge chest and the many, many scars there before she looks away shyly. I sigh and slip my shirt on, not wanting to embarrass her.

"Sorry," I grumble as she holds a plate to her chest, still not looking at me. "I'm dressed now," I tell her, and she peeks at me like she doesn't believe me, but when she sees my chest is covered, she swallows and licks her lips.

"I didn't mean to... erm, interrupt you," she blurts, her voice high-pitched. "I... uh... brought you some cookies." She thrusts the plate at me, and I take it, arching my eyebrow as I lift the tinfoil to see chocolate chip cookies underneath.

Is this what normal people do?

"Thanks," I grumble, and then we just stare at each other. Do people invite each other in at this point? I'm not sure. I'm not good at this civilian life. I scrub the back of my head as she nods and starts to back away.

"You're welcome. Will we see you at the town meeting tonight?" she inquires.

"Maybe," I mutter.

She smiles shyly and glances away before looking back at me. "I hope I do." She scurries to her car and rushes down my long, private driveway that has nothing but forest surrounding it. The driveway isn't even marked.

I wanted to disappear, and I did.

It took me a while to find a town I deemed suitable. It had to have enough exits and places to disappear, as well as a lack of technology, like cameras, and a big enough population so although they know I'm here, I won't stand out too much. It worked, and I found a place on the edge of the forest. The locals are wary and tend to avoid me, but that's fine, because I avoid them too. Bessie is the only one who comes out here. I found her when she hurt her foot hiking in the woods after she bought the property a couple of miles up the road. I helped her to my truck before taking her to her house, and now she insists on trying to drag me into the idyllic village life of this little town I call home.

Shutting the door, I stare down at the cookies, unsure what to do with them. Was this just a nice gesture or a way of her trying to get to know me? She has been trying for a while, but such a sweet, shy little thing shouldn't look at me like that. I'll bring her nothing but heartache and pain.

She would not survive me.

I grab two and jam them into my mouth—not bad—before stripping my shirt off and getting back to removing these godawful yellow cabinets in the old-style kitchen. I knew this place was a fixer-upper when I bought it cash in hand. It's a good thing I got one that needs work, my little projects are all that keep me sane.

I had no idea how boring normal life would be.

*Civilian life isn't made for men like us…*

Donald's words echo in my head. Is he right?

But I can't go back now, not again, the cost is too high.

I paid the ultimate price for my freedom, for this life. I will never go back.

For anyone.

## CHAPTER TWO

Alena

"Fuck you! You cock-sucking piece of shit!" I shout, uselessly tugging on the chains, my voice raw from all my screaming. Blood steadily drips down my wrists from the shackles biting into my skin, which rips further with my movements.

My arms are dead after hanging in the air for so long, and my hair is matted and greasy, dangling in front of my face and irritating me. My once white tank top is filthy and sticks to my unbound chest with sweat. The white panties they put me in are covered in blood and other stains I'm trying not to think about, the high waistband cutting into my now bony hips. My legs are freezing, and my toes are equally as dirty as the rest of my body, the nails broken and chipped.

What else can you expect after months of captivity?

Crossing my legs, I try to capture some of the warmth rising from the wet stone floor that has become my life, my cell, for the last few months. They dragged me here after the sale went bad and I tried to kill my buyer, labelling me as trash, unworthy to put to work or sell again. Disfigured, they called me, from the scar my last master carved into my 'once pretty face' for all to see. They said they would just stick a paper bag on my head, since my body was still fuckable if they didn't look.

Yet every time they tried to sell me, I managed to wreck it, so eventually they grew bored and brought me in here—a toy for their men to use however they wished. I think they are trying to see how long it takes to kill me. They haven't fed me in over three days, giving me only tiny sips of water to keep me alive. But they won't kill me, I won't give them the pleasure.

"You hear me? You won't kill me! When I get free, you're dead! All of you!" I scream, my voice breaking. Tears would fill my eyes if I had more water in my body, or would they? It's been so long since I've cried, and it's a useless waste of time. It didn't stop them from taking me.

Raping me.

Selling me.

Torturing me.

Disfiguring me.

Useless, that's what tears are, just like me.

I hang here, the time passing strangely. I can't tell if it's morning or night anymore, never mind what day or month it is. All I know are these four walls, the rats scurrying about in the corner, sometimes biting my toes, the water dripping from the holey roof, and the breeze coming in through the high barred window behind me. My arms are chained to the left and right wall, pulled tight in the air and spread so wide I don't even know if I would be able to use them anymore.

A noise has me lifting my head sluggishly. "Hello? Is someone there?" I call and then freeze. Fear flows through me, followed by self-hatred and disgust as the door opens, revealing Ken. His thick face is twisted up in a sneer, his hands going to the belt as he pulls it free from his trousers, his sausage fingers fumbling with the movements. He's not the smartest tool in the box, but he sure is a mean bastard.

He steps closer, his boots loud on the stone. "Miss me, creature?"

"Fuck you, limp dick!" I spit at him, laughing when he recoils in disgust as it hits his face. There's one thing I've learned since I've been down here—once you are broken, truly violated, there isn't much you can't survive. I quickly grew used to the pain, and excitement courses through me at the thought of hurting this man.

"You'll pay for that," he snaps.

Good, it's better than him sticking that sorry excuse for a cock inside me. I know if I get him mad enough, he'll just torture me instead. The belt whips out, slapping across my thigh, and I thrash in my chains, pain surging through my body as he hits me with it again and again, the buckle ripping through my skin. I can't even scream anymore, and eventually, I pass out.

A mercy.

When I wake up, he's gone.

Blood trickles steadily down my legs, joining the dripping water as it hits the stone below me. It's just more scars to add to my body. I have lost count of how many they have given me.

If I ever escape, I know I will have to hide away. People will recoil at my appearance, but to me, my body and scars prove I survived. They represent each time I fought to come back, even when the world was against me.

One night, one stupid night brought me here.

I was flirting with a handsome club owner, trying to make my ex jealous, and when we went to his office, he drugged me. I fought as hard as I could, but I was still taken.

I wasn't strong enough.

Now I am.

I will never let them surprise me again. They can torture me, use me, and break my body repeatedly, but I will never be weak or trusting again. I will get free, and then I will hunt them down one by one and kill them all for what they did to me.

For all the girls they have taken.

I will get my revenge.

# CHAPTER THREE

Idris

I stare around at the pub Bessie kept inviting me to until I finally gave in. Maybe it's because I'm worried I made a mistake, but I'm going to try to make being a civilian work. She said she owed me a drink for saving her. I didn't think so, but I have to try and fit in. With my frame and scars, I already stand out in the quiet village, and even more so now in the local pub. I have to duck my head to get into the small corner pub. Old green booths line the walls with slot machines and sticky tables between them. There is a dark wood bar curving around the interior with an older lady serving two old men wearing flat caps.

I scan everyone in a second, looking for a weapon or any threats. When I find none, I head to the booth where Bessie is sitting with an older lady, giggling and talking. I tower over the table, and the old lady actually gasps as I stand there. I tuck my hands into my pockets to make me look less intimidating and to be close to my weapon—a habit.

Bessie smiles at me though, even as she averts her eyes so she doesn't meet my gaze. "Hi! I'm so glad you came!" she gushes, and the old lady looks me up and down.

"Holy cowboy, are you a giant or something? You look like those

American football players. Doesn't he, girl?" she asks, nudging Bessie who giggles.

"I guess," she murmurs softly.

"I'm big," is all I say before I grab the wooden seat, grimacing as I try to sit without breaking it. It looks old and fragile, not something that should be around my lumbering frame.

I hear a creak, but luckily, it doesn't break as I sit there looking between them. I chose the only chair with my back to the wall so I can see every entrance and exit—another habit. The silence stretches on. Bessie doesn't talk, and I don't know what to say. I've never dealt with girls like her before. She's shy, and the ones I'm used to shoot and ask questions later and tend to be very... mouthy.

It puts me on edge as I awkwardly sit here with her not looking at me.

"Do you want a drink?" she asks suddenly, and I turn my head to catch her eyes. For a moment, she holds my gaze, but eventually, she drops her eyes to the table.

"I don't drink," I tell her.

"Then why come to a pub, my lad?" The older lady cackles.

"I was invited. Google said it was rude to ignore the invitation," I grumble, and Bessie giggles again like I'm hilarious. I frown, wondering what I said that was funny.

We sit there awkwardly for an hour before I decide I've had enough social time and go to leave. Bessie jumps up. "I'll walk back with you," she says hurriedly, and I frown but nod as she grabs a jacket and slips into it, waving at the older lady before following me outside.

We walk side by side along the cobbled streets, the sun setting over the hills as we do. It's an idyllic town, very picturesque, the perfect place to retire to. But I'm beginning to understand that men like me aren't made to sit still. Even now, I'm alert, looking, watching, and wondering if that will ever disappear.

The entire walk is silent, and I stop before her quaint little house where she fidgets nervously before leaning up and kissing my cheek, surprising me. "Thank you for coming," she murmurs with a meek smile and a blush. My cock doesn't twitch, even as the heat from the kiss soaks into my scarred skin.

Too innocent, too pure… She couldn't handle the things I do.

Maybe that's why I'm not attracted to her. She's beautiful, that's for sure, but that's never been enough. I need them to fight, to be strong… to be confident and stand up to me. I've never found anyone who could. The few nights I spend with women are enough to make them fear me and enough to sate my lust, if only slightly.

I need that spark that burns into an inferno, and she doesn't have it.

I nod, and her smile dims as she turns and rushes through her door. I watch from outside in the dark like the monster I am. With a disgusted sneer on my lips, which is aimed at myself, I turn and head home.

No, Bessie is better staying as far away from me as she possibly can.

After all, they don't call me Boogeyman for nothing.

# CHAPTER FOUR

### Alena

I know what they are going to do. I would rather not know or feel it though, so I yank myself forward, choking on the restraints. I stopped caring about their names weeks or maybe even months ago. I call these two Small Dick One and Small Dick Two. They like to work together. One likes to watch while the other plays—it's what gets them off. Unlike some of the others, they don't just want my body, they don't just want to satiate their lust and let their cum drip from my lifeless, ruined form.

No, they want my pain.

They want my screams, and they usually get them. I may be strong, stronger than I ever thought possible, but I always break. They find new ways to rip the agony from my throat in animalistic howls. They laugh, stroking themselves as they hurt me, and only when I've passed out and been revived after hours of torture do they finally give in.

They take my body at the same time, leaving me bloodied, scarred, and dripping with their release. Those are the days and nights in which I would kill for the drugs the other girls get to numb the sensations. Fuck, just a shower to remove the feel of their hands.

I get none of that.

If they are here now, though, it means they have pleased the boss. He doesn't let them loose on me often, hell, on any of the girls. Their tastes are too violent, and it usually kills them… all except me.

Their favourite fucking pet.

"She's so messed up." Small Dick One laughs as I choke, my vision blackening as my lungs scream for air.

*Please let me pass out, please let me avoid even some of the pain and humiliation to come.* I always think I can't sink lower, that I can't become more of an animal than I already am.

When you strip away the fancy clothes, makeup, hair, and jewels, that's all we are.

We are animals just trying to survive, and they have taken me down to rock bottom.

I stretch harder, determined. They want my screams? Fine, but tonight, they will have to work harder for them. I'll hurt, choke, and kill myself before they leave my throat tonight. I smile at him as I finally pass out, my last thought being, *Thank God I don't have to be awake for this.*

---

I didn't pass out long enough. I'm just rousing when they toss a bottle of piss over my head. The stench makes me gag as it runs down my face and body, soaking my hair so the wet tendrils dangle over my shoulders. When I open my eyes, they water, and I have to blink through it to see them both smirking at me.

"There's our favourite pet. Hope you don't mind that we got started without you," Small Dick Two taunts with a laugh.

Panting, heart racing, I look down at my body, even as dread fills me at what they could have done while I was out. A small part of me is almost laughing at the fact they did it while I was unconscious so I couldn't scream, knowing I deprived them of that.

My heart stops in my chest and triples in speed when I observe the damage, which, of course, only makes my blood pump harder. I'm surprised I even have enough left in my body to, but shit. They cut long, clean slices down my legs. There is an inch between each slice, from ankle to hips. How the fuck did I not feel that?

Is my body dying? Am I finally so used to pain that I can ignore it now?

Or is my entire body an aching, rotting wound, so one more drop of pain is insignificant?

My hands are still chained, and I can't feel them anymore, like two dead weights. My toes scrape across the floor as I jerk my legs to see if I can feel them. They are cold to the bone, even as my bright red blood trails down them. I watch in rapt fascination as it slithers through the dirt like a snake to reveal pale, pink tender skin underneath, then it slides across my foot and toe to eventually drip to the floor.

I hear the buzz of their voices, but I concentrate on that steady stream of blood until a fist grabs my hair and yanks my head back painfully, ripping strands free. Small Dick Two gets in my face with an evil twist of his lips as Small Dick One sneers behind him. "Wakey, wakey, pet. Don't go dying on us yet, we haven't even had our fun."

My mouth is dry, so dry, yet I swirl it around and manage to form enough saliva to spit right in his face. He recoils with a snarl, and I laugh, my head falling forward from exhaustion and malnourishment, yet I still laugh, the sound high-pitched and crazy.

"Small dicks, small dicks, couldn't get it up without the pain. Small dicks, small dicks, gotta rape to get pussy!" I carry on singing until they get angry.

*Good one, Alena, piss off the men torturing you.*

But I can't stop, even as they take their fury out on my body. I laugh through it, each bead of pain bringing me closer to death, to the darkness I will never give in to. Before I die, I will get revenge, and each touch, each scar, each stab of agony moving through me is simply another reason for me to fight.

For me to stay.

For me to get my revenge.

My eye is swelling from their fists, my lip is busted, and my cheeks are split open when they step back. I lick my lip and taste my blood, which is undoubtedly coating my teeth, and I grin, almost snarling like a wild animal. "That all you got?" I croak out. "Pussy."

Small Dick One's eyes darken further, and I know I've pushed them too far.

I might actually die tonight. It won't be about fighting to survive, it will be about fighting that warm embrace coming for me.

I swallow and tilt my chin back, refusing to beg, refusing to scream. "Shall we?" he murmurs, and I incline my head, trying to retain some dignity.

"Let's."

He turns and takes a long black board from the table they must have brought in with them. With it in hand, he gives it a few practice swings before grinning at me. Prior to all this, I used to like a few kinky things in the bedroom, and it reminds me of that... only so much fucking worse. There are no safe words, no aftercare, only pain.

Always pain.

He brings it down across my stomach, and I curl inwards, losing my breath as he smacks it across my arms in rapid succession, which I can finally feel again. The burning agony, however, is starting to make me wish I couldn't. He slams it into my legs, back, and ass over and over. None of my skin is left untouched, bar my face. I'm panting and still not screaming, but my tongue is bleeding from my teeth and the force of me restraining my own howls of pain.

They take it as a challenge. Small Dick One picks a long flogger next, only the ends of this one are sharp and tipped with metal. He walks around me, and I hunch, knowing what's coming. I try not to brace, to tense, to make the pain worse, but I can't help it.

When I hear it whizz through the air, I struggle forward, but it connects with my skin anyway, slicing through my unmarred flesh. Blood instantly flows down my back to my ass and legs. It's warm, unlike me. Small Dick Two gets in my face, staring into my eyes as the flogger is brought down again and again, crisscrossing lashes on my back until I feel my flesh being ripped apart.

Raw meat and blood cover me, and when he starts on my legs, I can't hold back.

I howl in pain, right into Small Dicks Two's face, the sound choked and raw. Like an animal, he groans and smashes his lips to mine, tasting my defeat, my blood, and my life. I bite him, even in my hazy state, and he rips away, tearing his own lips. His eyes are wild as he reaches for his jeans and unbuttons them, pulling out his—yep, you guessed it—small dick and starting to stroke as he looks over my bloodied frame.

I focus over his shoulder, trying to block the pain, but he doesn't let me as he grabs my thighs and wrenches them up. Small Dick One holds them for him, even as I struggle, and those tattered panties are torn away, leaving me bare. My pussy is cold and dry, but he doesn't care. He lines up and slams into me, ripping me.

The agony echoes through me until I scream and scream. It's been done before, but it never stops being the worst thing that can happen. My body is being taken, violated. He grunts as he fucks me. Blood drips from my core as his cock slams in and out of my tight channel. Small Dick One holds me, fingering the cuts on my leg to make them bleed as I feel his cock press against my ass. I close my eyes, letting myself be taken away. I'm not here.

*I'm somewhere else, anywhere else.*

I see my friends, my family. It's warm, and I'm not hungry. The sun hits my face, my belly is full, and laughter fills the air, but then I'm brought back when Small Dick One takes my asshole.

I'm thrown into my body, cold, in pain, and alone in the dark. The water drips to the floor in time with my blood, my heart rate erratic and my belly rolling as I debate throwing up on them, though there isn't anything to vomit.

I'm so cold, so very tired, yet I twist my hands in the manacles, cutting them to add to the pain to keep me alive, to keep me feeling so I'm unwilling to give in.

Small Dick One's grunts fill my ears, his hands gripping my legs and ass as he rams into me from behind until my body is one giant throbbing wound. Small Dick Two's hips stutter, and with a dog-like grunt, he comes, filling me with his sticky release before pulling out and squirting it across my legs and belly, and then he stumbles back with a satisfied smile.

I know I'll be left like this. I swallow, keeping my eyes on him as Small Dick One finds his release, slamming into my ass and filling it. He, too, pulls out, and I feel it drip from me. I almost cry at the sensation, at the pain, at the knowledge in their eyes. I ache to scrub my skin, to throw up their taste, to burn it out of me. But I can't.

I'll be left to hang in my blood and their filth. They might send a doctor in a few days to make sure I'm not dead and stitch up my wounds, but until then...

"Nice playing with you, pet. See you later!" they call. At least this was faster than normal. The door slams shut and locks behind them, and I sag, letting my hair cover my face as I blink back my tears.

I will not cry, even as my ass and pussy pump agony and hate through me. I let myself feel every inch, every ruined molecule of my body, so that when I get free—and I will—I will remember this and make them feel it twice as much.

I'll rip them to pieces. I'll rape them with objects like they did me. I'll cut their skin, deprive them of water and food. I'll torture them, and when they break, and they will, I won't stop.

I will make them nothing but animals.

Like me.

# CHAPTER FIVE

### Idris

I hear the crunch of tires on gravel and the roar of an engine before my cameras and alarm system even alert me to someone's approach—not that whoever it is would know they have triggered it. I hid the sensors underground and the cameras in trees along my entrance and both emergency exits.

I made this place a fortress before I even made it a home.

I'm awake and alert in a moment. Barefoot and wearing jeans, I tuck a gun into the back of my pants and slip two knives in my pockets, but when the loud knock comes at the door and I look at the camera, I sigh and sag. The adrenaline fades, but only slightly, because I can never be too careful.

It's the police.

I open the door and stare down at the two short, uniformed men, wondering what they want. They can't know who or what I am, and technically, I'm not even alive. I'm a ghost under a false name, and they would only ever even start to learn what a monster I am if they possessed a level five clearance.

No, this is something else. But what?

I keep the door partially closed and my hand on my gun—another fucking force of habit. I guess Donald was right—you can run, you can hide, but you can never take the training out of a soldier.

A spy.

An assassin.

"Yes?" I ask as politely as I can.

They fidget nervously, sharing a look before the one on the left, the older one, clears his throat and steps forward, trying to look serious and menacing even as I tower over him. Right now, my computers are bringing up everything on these men and informing me of anything I need to know. I've dealt with warlords, kings, spies, and assassins. Two local cops don't even make me blink.

"We need to ask you some questions."

"Why?" I growl.

They share another look, annoying me. I wish they would just get on with it. Can't they tell I want to be left alone?

"A local woman has gone missing, and you were the last person to be seen with her," he blurts out.

I jolt at that, narrowing my eyes on him. "Who?" I question, even though I know.

"Miss Bessie," he begins, and I see red.

Bessie is missing?

"Tell me everything," I demand.

"Erm, sir, this is an active investigation, but if you could answer our questions," he hedges nervously.

"I walked her home. She went inside at 8:05pm. I haven't seen her since. I have security cameras here, which register my comings and goings, and no, I will not give you the tape unless you have a warrant, as I'm not a suspect. Now tell me what happened to her," I snarl, giving up the pretence of being nice. They swallow and step back, seeing the change.

Seeing the true me.

Boogeyman, the hunter, the killer.

"We don't know. You're sure you didn't see or hear anything?" he queries, and I have to give him a bit of respect for continuing the questioning even though he's terrified.

"No."

"Okay, well, if you remember anything at all, you know where we are." With that, they nod at me and return to their car. I stand in the doorway, watching them quietly retreat. Their tires squeal and gravel sprays from their hurried exit, and a cool calm fills me.

Whoever has taken Bessie is going to regret it.

---

I'M AT HER HOUSE WITHIN THE HOUR. I WAIT FOR THE POLICE TO depart, leaving only tape around the structure. Fucking idiots didn't even check the area or bring in CSI. I break in through the back. The door is wood and easy enough to get through. I only have to duck under the tape and pick the lock, which means whoever took her didn't use this as an entry point. I slide through the dark, stepping quietly over broken glass in the kitchen. Using my torch, I examine the scene. Chairs are overturned, and blood trails lead to the entryway where the lock is broken and the door is busted in.

They came in and took her unaware while she was drinking in the kitchen. She put up a fight, but not much. There were two, maybe three, from the boot prints. Military grade boots.

Retracing my steps, I check every inch, even getting on my knees, and that's when I see it. Hidden beneath the sofa, clearly dropped and kicked under there, is a phone. I pull it free. It's a simple burner, and the screen is busted and won't turn on.

I pocket it, knowing exactly where I need to take it, and with one more look around, I leave as silently as I came, like I was never here.

My trip back to my cottage is quick. I throw my emergency EVAC bag and weapons into my car and speed out of the small village, leaving the silence behind as I drive to the city.

Two hours later, I'm outside of his mansion. He lets me through the gates, and when I pull up outside, the door opens. Spider is framed in the entrance, his woman behind him. She nods at me and retreats after kissing his cheek. He's the best, one of Donald's men... a man I used to work with before this. Before I became a ghost.

"You're supposed to be dead, remember?" he snaps. "Retiring means no surprise visits. It means lying low—"

"I need your help," I grind out, the words almost painful. A warrior knows when to ask for assistance, but I never did like owing this man anything. He tends to collect, and never in a way you want.

That surprises him enough to nod and allow me in. He takes me to the living room and remains standing, watching me. I don't waste time, pulling the phone free and thrusting it at him. "You're the best hacker I know. I need to know what's on this."

"Why?" he asks with a frown, but a cold, calculating curiosity gleams in his eyes. I wouldn't fuck with him. What that man can do with a computer is terrifying, not to mention what he's capable of with his hands. He's an expert at wet work, and we share a strong respect for each other. Hell, he even helped me get out of the game, so if I'm here now, he understands it's serious.

He sighs, knowing I won't answer. "Stay here." He takes the stairs two at a time. I wait with my hands in my pockets. My eyes flicker around, but I remain respectful. I hear some muttering, no doubt from his woman, and then ten minutes later, he's back downstairs.

"Burner cell, bought at a shop in the city two nights ago by cash. There was a camera outside, it was a Middle Eastern man, ID ran." He thrusts some paper at me. "There's the address and car make and model. It's currently inactive and nowhere on traffic cameras. There is this too. I tracked it back as far as I could. His last stop was an abandoned warehouse on the east side. It used to be owned by a newspaper company, but now it's empty." He passes it all over and shoves his hands in his pockets, watching me.

"Are you back?" Three simple words, but they hold a lot of questions and meaning. If I say yes, then I'm back in this world. There will be no getting free again, and I have already sacrificed and fought enough to do just that. You don't just turn your back on the Clergy, you don't just walk free from being an assassin, yet I did.

The only man in history to do so.

"No, this is just an errand. A day or two, then I will be gone again." I incline my head. "Thank you for the information, I owe you."

He waves it away. "Go then, I don't want payment, only this." He steps closer, his eyes narrowed. "Disappear. Go back to wherever the fuck you went to find peace. Not just for your welfare and my own work's sake—I don't have time to make you disappear again—but there is shit going down in the city we can't have you in the middle of, understood?"

I nod, and without another word, I head back through the house and out of the front door. We may be respectful to one another, but we aren't friends. We are just two monsters who live in the same darkness. It was a courtesy warning, and I need to make sure I heed it. I don't want to piss him or Donald off, not after everything.

I told him I wasn't back…

*It was a lie.*

I'm retired, I'm supposed to be dead, yet I know I can't walk away. She was kind to me, and for that, I owe her my loyalty. She did not align herself with me because of what I'm capable of or out of obligation, she did it out of kindness, something I'm not used to.

The police will never find her. I know that.

No, this is my duty. I know the horrors she could be experiencing right now. As a woman, and an innocent one at that, she would never survive, she isn't strong enough. I have to find her before whoever took her breaks her, if only for my peace of mind. How could I start my new life knowing the one person who has been kind to me, welcoming, is being tortured, even killed, and I could have helped? I can't. My mind would never let me rest. Already, I feel anger and hatred clawing at me, demanding blood.

Boogeyman is back, and he's on the hunt.

God save the poor bastards who get in my way.

# CHAPTER SIX

### Alena

The door is wrenched open. I don't even lift my head until ice-cold water is tossed over me, making me gasp as I shudder and curl in on myself. The filth, blood, and cum is washed away as another bucket is thrown over me.

Like a wild animal, I snarl at them, struggling in my chains as I blink through the water to see the two guards standing there. They laugh and ignore me as they glance at each other. "That will do. Get her chained and bring her upstairs, they are waiting," one orders and storms away, leaving me with a big bastard who marches into my cell.

Even if I could take him, if my body wasn't dying, what would I do?

He unclips me from the ceiling, and I fall to the floor with a grunt, smacking into the dirty, wet stones with an audible bang. I flip onto my back with a groan, wiggling my toes and hands to get some circulation going, but he grabs me, wrenches me to my feet, and ties my chains together before turning and starting to pull me from my cell.

My legs give way. I don't have enough energy, and it's been too long since I've used them, so he ends up dragging me down the darkened corridor. What's happening? Where are we going? I want to ask, but I know I won't get an answer, so I twist in his grip and yank on the chains. My hips, ass, and legs hit the floor painfully as I struggle.

Threats and words leave my lips as he uses my hands to pick me up before dragging me up the stairs. My hair falls into my eyes, obscuring my vision, and then a door is opened and a bright light hits my face, making me recoil as it blinds me through my greasy locks.

Light… When was the last time I saw light?

I don't have time to appreciate it though. I'm towed quickly down a corridor. Yelling and laughter reaches me, and then I'm tossed into a darkened room again.

"Fucking waste of supplies," the man mutters as he glares down at me. He grips my hair and lifts my head, revealing my face. "Such a shame they ruined you." He chuckles and then unlocks my wrists and steps back.

I struggle to my feet to try and escape, and he laughs like he knows my thoughts. My legs shake and collapse, leaving me helpless as he slams the door shut and takes that last sliver of light with him.

What's going to happen now?

They have never pulled me from my cell. Is this it? Is this when they try to kill me?

Let them.

---

I don't know how long I'm left in here, but I force myself to stretch and walk, no matter how often I fall. I do star jumps and try to complete some push-ups, but my arms shake and give out.

I'm too weak.

I used to love working out, being strong. Fuck, I was a weightlifter, now look at me. Disgusted, I search the room, finding a tray of food and water. I force myself to eat the stale bread and cold stew. It'll provide the nutrients my body needs to get my revenge.

After eating, I piss in the corner like an animal and then continue to stretch. I don't stop moving, forcing my limbs to work normally again, even if they do shake slightly. Eventually, I tire and sit down, not wanting to use all my energy. I'm going to need it to get free.

About ten minutes later, the door opens again, and I jump to my feet as quickly as I can. Without even looking, I throw myself at them, fighting and biting like a wild animal. It takes all four of them to restrain me. Panting, I hang between them at an awkward angle.

"Fucking wild cunt bit me," one of them snarls.

"If the boss knew we almost got taken down by this twat..." Another groans.

"Shut up, let's just get her to the pit," another replies, and they become quiet. I relax in their grip, not wanting to hurt myself. They are taking me somewhere—the pit? What's that? I guess I'll find out. Maybe there will be a chance to escape then.

I'm lifted and carried down the corridor, down more stairs, and manoeuvred through more twists and turns than I can count. The voices and laughter grow louder, music too, which pumps through the walls and floors in time with my racing heart.

I'm thrown through a door with a rising metal gate. It slams shut behind me, and I hear cheers. Spinning, I push to my feet, and my mouth drops open as I look up and around.

I'm in a dirt pit, a literal pit. Concrete walls, at least twenty feet high, circle the space. There are blood, nail marks, and stains across the grey cement that make me swallow in fear. But it's the people that have me shuffling backwards nervously. What is this?

There are stands, chairs, sofas, and loungers circling the pit in tiered seating, which are all filled with women in fancy dresses and men in suits. Jewels sparkle on their necks, ears, and hands. Their hair is perfectly done and styled, and their makeup is impeccably applied.

Chandeliers hang from the ceiling as the music switches to something more upbeat. Champagne and wine are served on small trays by naked women with collars around their necks. I spot a few more seated on the floor like dogs in front of couples, men, and even an older woman.

Bile rises in my throat. It's a fucking party... and it looks like I'm the entertainment.

## CHAPTER SEVEN

### Idris

I go to the warehouse Spider found. If that's the last place the car was seen, it's more than likely they will be there. Just as I pull up into the overgrown lot outside, surrounded by trees and a broken chain-link fence, my phone rings.

I glance at the number and sigh, knowing I have to answer it if I want to survive another thirty seconds in his city. I press the green button and leave him on speaker as I move my seat back and begin to check my weapons, knowing I could find anything in there. "Well, hello to you too," he greets after a moment of silence.

"What?" I snap, and he laughs, used to my attitude and unfazed by it.

"A little spider told me you were in town." He pauses, but I don't speak. "Do I need to be worried?"

"No."

"Good, remember what it took to get you out," he murmurs. "Whatever you're up to, you have our support, but keep the bloodshed and mayhem to a minimum. If you draw attention, we might not be able to keep your status as a ghost." He hangs up, knowing better than to wait for a response. Grunting, I push my phone into my pocket and slide out.

He's right. I need to do this silently. Get her, kill them, and then disappear again. I'm a ghost for a reason, and seeing my handiwork on TV will only bring my enemies back down on me. I worked too fucking hard to get out. I can still do this and secure my freedom.

I can.

The warehouse towers above me as I pull out my gun, flipping off the safety and checking there's one in the chamber before I quickly and quietly move closer. Poking my head around the side of the brick building, I spot the car Spider mentioned. It's off, and when I reach it, I press my hand to the hood. It's cold, so they've been here a while.

There's a peeling blue metal door before it. I try the handle and find it unlocked. Swinging it open slowly, I step into the darkened warehouse and make sure the door doesn't slam shut and alert anyone. The floor is made of uneven, dirty concrete, and there are cages hanging from the ceiling. I duck behind one, scanning the area. There's an old CCTV camera in the corner, but it isn't on. On the back wall is a stage with cameras pointed at it and flood lights, but they are also off, and I don't see anyone.

So where are they?

I hear a quiet shuffle behind me and spin too late. I'm rusty. The gun clicks as he flicks off the safety and presses it to my forehead. A moment later, I feel another pressed to the back of my head. "Hello, Boogeyman. We've been waiting for you." He grins.

I lift my hand and drop my gun, letting them assume I'm giving in. He starts to relax, so I quickly snap my hands out, smashing my right fist into his wrist while my left slams into the gun, freeing it from his grip. I quickly shoot him in the knee, turning to avoid the second gun and firing blindly into the chest of the man behind me. He goes down and I whirl back. The first man is on the floor, screaming and clutching his bleeding knee. Lifting my foot, I press it against his wound and wait until his screams of agony die down.

"Waiting for me? Why?" I growl out.

When he doesn't answer, I dig my boot in deeper. His face pales, so I lean down and slap him. "No passing out. Why were you waiting for me?" Fuck, I wish I had my tools, but I don't have time to torture this fucker. It's clear this was a setup.

But by whom? And why? How did they know I would be coming for her?

"It's a trap," he grits out through clenched, bloodied teeth. "Fucking moron."

I smash my boot into his leg and snap it. He howls then passes out, and I shoot him and turn away, bending to pick up my gun when I hear an engine. I check my gun, and I'm just stepping forward when I feel a light breath across my neck. Before I can turn, something sinks into the side of my neck. A sharp poke. Turning with a snarl, I yank the needle free and shoot the man but stumble.

My body is becoming sluggish, and my eyes and hearing are starting to turn fuzzy. Fuck. I look at the needle. What did they put in it? I fall forward, catching myself on a cage which rings out loudly, giving away my position. Blind and deaf, I try to make my way towards the door. I need to get out of here and find somewhere safe to lie low while the drug pumps through my system. My heart is already racing from the fight, so I try to slow it, concentrating on my breathing as I stagger across the uneven concrete floor.

I spot the door before me, the hazy blue my destination. I fall into it, smacking my hand into the handle over and over again uselessly as darkness closes in on me. Fuck no. I snarl and try again, managing to hook my numb hand in the handle just before the darkness eclipses my vision.

I pass out.

# CHAPTER EIGHT

### Alena

"For tonight's entertainment, we have our scarred house dog," a voice announces over the speakers. As I turn, something jabs me from behind the gate, pushing me, and I stumble forward into the sand. "Isn't she an ugly cunt? Strong fighter though. She's been serving our men's... appetites for four months now!" Laughter and cheers go up as I clench my fists, snarling at them.

They dare judge me?

They dare mock me?

"And fighting our dog is our newest little virgin. If she survives... well, she will be free for everyone!" The voice laughs. Fight? Virgin?

Then it clicks. They are going to make me fight someone else. This is what this is—a fucking fighting ring. They're cock fighting, but for humans. What the fuck? I don't know why it shocks me. They traffic girls, they get them addicted to drugs, they rape and torture them... Why should this be any different?

A crank sounds, and I turn to see another gate opposite mine. A crying, fighting, screaming, skinny blonde is shoved into the pit. She lands hard on the ground, curling into a ball as she sobs. Her body shakes from the force. She's in a see-through, white nightie, which is torn with some blood spotted across it. Her long blonde hair is tangled and concealing her face.

I glare at the gate and rush to her side, dropping next to her. "Are you okay?" I murmur, reaching out to touch her skin. She recoils with a scream, scrambling across the dirt.

Her blue eyes are wide and bloodshot, and tears cascade across her pale, stained cheeks. Her lips tremble as she stares at me, her gaze broken and almost empty. I can see she's shattering, or maybe she's already gone and withdrawn into herself and this is just a knee-jerk reaction.

I saw it in the girls when I was first taken. There were those who could survive the abuse, not just body wise but in the mind. Then there were those who couldn't, whose minds fractured as they hid inside themselves to avoid feeling anything, leaving them numb and empty.

Broken beyond repair.

I stay crouched with my hand out like I'm talking to a wild animal. She stares back, running her eyes across my scarred face with a flinch. I wince a little at that. I know I look horrendous, scary from the scars, but the fact she reacted like that hurts a part of me I thought was unable to be wounded anymore.

"I won't hurt you," I assure her.

"Look at our dog, trying to save the girl," a voice calls, and I flinch before hardening and ignoring the laughter and teasing comments as they watch us. This may be their entertainment, but for me, this is my nightmare.

I can survive my own torture, my own violation, and I can stop myself from breaking, but seeing an innocent, young girl being tortured and used as bait for me?

It makes me angry, angrier than I have ever been.

It's that quiet, slow burning fury that means someone will die soon, but I keep my face calm and my gaze on her as she tries to cover her chest to hide her little rosy nipples pressing against the fabric. What have they done to her to put that much fear and detachment there? I dread to think about it. So much can be done while still keeping a woman 'pure.' As they told me once, the pure girls go for more money.

The rich fuckers pay to take their virginity.

# CHAPTER EIGHT

## Alena

"For tonight's entertainment, we have our scarred house dog," a voice announces over the speakers. As I turn, something jabs me from behind the gate, pushing me, and I stumble forward into the sand. "Isn't she an ugly cunt? Strong fighter though. She's been serving our men's… appetites for four months now!" Laughter and cheers go up as I clench my fists, snarling at them.

They dare judge me?

They dare mock me?

"And fighting our dog is our newest little virgin. If she survives… well, she will be free for everyone!" The voice laughs. Fight? Virgin?

Then it clicks. They are going to make me fight someone else. This is what this is—a fucking fighting ring. They're cock fighting, but for humans. What the fuck? I don't know why it shocks me. They traffic girls, they get them addicted to drugs, they rape and torture them… Why should this be any different?

A crank sounds, and I turn to see another gate opposite mine. A crying, fighting, screaming, skinny blonde is shoved into the pit. She lands hard on the ground, curling into a ball as she sobs. Her body shakes from the force. She's in a see-through, white nightie, which is torn with some blood spotted across it. Her long blonde hair is tangled and concealing her face.

I glare at the gate and rush to her side, dropping next to her. "Are you okay?" I murmur, reaching out to touch her skin. She recoils with a scream, scrambling across the dirt.

Her blue eyes are wide and bloodshot, and tears cascade across her pale, stained cheeks. Her lips tremble as she stares at me, her gaze broken and almost empty. I can see she's shattering, or maybe she's already gone and withdrawn into herself and this is just a knee-jerk reaction.

I saw it in the girls when I was first taken. There were those who could survive the abuse, not just body wise but in the mind. Then there were those who couldn't, whose minds fractured as they hid inside themselves to avoid feeling anything, leaving them numb and empty.

Broken beyond repair.

I stay crouched with my hand out like I'm talking to a wild animal. She stares back, running her eyes across my scarred face with a flinch. I wince a little at that. I know I look horrendous, scary from the scars, but the fact she reacted like that hurts a part of me I thought was unable to be wounded anymore.

"I won't hurt you," I assure her.

"Look at our dog, trying to save the girl," a voice calls, and I flinch before hardening and ignoring the laughter and teasing comments as they watch us. This may be their entertainment, but for me, this is my nightmare.

I can survive my own torture, my own violation, and I can stop myself from breaking, but seeing an innocent, young girl being tortured and used as bait for me?

It makes me angry, angrier than I have ever been.

It's that quiet, slow burning fury that means someone will die soon, but I keep my face calm and my gaze on her as she tries to cover her chest to hide her little rosy nipples pressing against the fabric. What have they done to her to put that much fear and detachment there? I dread to think about it. So much can be done while still keeping a woman 'pure.' As they told me once, the pure girls go for more money.

The rich fuckers pay to take their virginity.

"Now listen up, dog," the voice says, and I lift my head, glaring around. They are all staring. "Hurt the girl, kill her, and you win yourself a day's reprieve from our tender touches." The crowd breaks out into raucous laughter.

The gate starts to rise and I spin, pushing to my feet in a moment. I stand before her, my legs spread and fists clenched, prepared to defend her, but a man simply tosses a knife into the dirt at my feet and the gate closes again. She's crying softly now, and when I look down, she's rocking back and forth.

"Kill her and save yourself."

They all watch and take bets, wondering if I'll do it, if I'll kill her to save myself. I stand there staring, unmoving.

"Do it, dog, or we'll rape her in front of you and make her our new little toy instead of you." I flinch, knowing they will. Can I really give up a day's peace for a stranger when all it will do is bring us both pain?

Grabbing the knife, I drop to my knees and lift her head, then I press the cool metal to her throat. The cheers get louder, but I block them out. I stare into her eyes and flinch. I can't do it, I can't kill her even to save myself. Even to stop her from having to go through what I did.

I just can't.

"No." I go to stand, to drop the knife, but her fragile hand shoots out, and with more strength than I thought she possessed, she grips my wrist. For a moment, something akin to a person flashes in those glassy blue depths.

"Kill me," she begs quietly, so low they can't hear.

I flinch, and she blinks sluggishly. "Please, kill me. I won't survive this, kill me. Set me free."

"What?" I snap, trying to pull back without hurting her. "I'm not fucking killing you."

"It's me or you. You're stronger than me, I see it in your eyes. I couldn't survive…" She looks me over. "This. Kill me, or I'll do it myself."

She's made her choice. She would rather die than let them touch her, rather die than fight. She's given up and is looking for a way out.

She presses herself closer to the blade. I pull it back slightly, trying to stop her, but she's determined. She wants to kill herself.

"I'm not strong enough," she whispers. "Please."

"Do it, do it," the crowd chants.

"End her!"

"Rip out her heart!"

"Gut her!"

"Fuck her corpse!"

Tears fill my eyes at what awaits us both. She sobs harder, retreating back into herself. She's weak, too weak to survive. The screams get louder and louder, and she covers her ears, shouting at me to do it. Everything blurs, my heart slows, and my hands shake.

"Do it!" she yells, repeating it over and over, and it gets to be too much.

I snap.

I slice her throat in one move. I move so swiftly, I don't even have time to think until I'm standing there with the blood-coated knife in my grasp. Her eyes widen, and her mouth opens and closes as her neck squirts blood. Her hands come up to cover the wound, to instinctively save herself, but that will only prolong her death and make her suffer. So even though my heart shrivels and tears drip down my face, I let the knife fall to the dirt, forgotten, staining it forever. I grab her hands and stop her from staunching the flow.

Her eyes lock on me, and I refuse to look away, even while a part of me withers at what I've just done. My mind blocks it out, refusing to admit I just killed this innocent little girl.

I took a life, and that will have to stay with me forever.

My eyes remain on her while her blood pumps from her body and covers us both. Slowly, her eyelids begin to shut, and only when she stops moving, stops breathing, do I lower her to the ground. I pull her dress down to try and cover her as much as I can and then sit back.

I stare at my hands, coated in crimson.

My tears drip steadily as I stare at her broken corpse. She looks like a marionette with her strings cut. Did I make the right choice? Am I as much of a monster as them now? I did what it took to survive, but in doing so, did I damn my soul?

I crack. My head tips back with an agony filled bellow.

They've done it, they've finally broken me. But in those dark, bloodied shards, I find something. I find the depths of my soul and what I'm willing to do.

Anything.

# CHAPTER NINE

### Idris

I wake up suddenly, a loud, jarring bang wrenching me from the warm blackness cocooning me. My head spins, my eyes aren't working, and my ears are ringing. My body is exhausted and sluggish, but I remember the needle, the warehouse, the drugging. Breathing through the sickness, I count backwards until my heart slows and my stomach stops rolling, then I force my eyes open to scan my location.

Whoever it was, they were prepared. They wanted me for a reason... but what?

The bang comes again, closer, like the sound of a metal door shutting, and then I hear keys in a lock and laughter as footsteps retreat, the voices fading also. "You heard the boss, she won her peace for the night fair and square. Go sink your dick into one of the other pieces of merchandise."

My eyes finally adjust to the dark, and I survey the small, damp cell I'm in. I tug on my hands, but they won't budge, so I lift my aching head to see they are chained to the ceiling. My arms are stretched out above me, but even so, my feet, also chained, touch the floor from my height. The clinking sound of my restraints as I move is loud. Snarling, I yank on them, testing their strength, but they don't dislodge.

My shirt is gone, and my abs and chest are covered in dirt, post drug sweat, and even some blood—not mine though. I don't feel any wounds unless they are small. My jeans are still in place and hanging low on my hips. My boots are gone, socks too, and I know they have taken all my weapons.

Who are they?

Only time will tell, so for now, I need to focus on learning everything about my location and who took me, and preparing my body for their return. They kidnapped the wrong man.

You don't fuck with Boogeyman.

I hear a muffled voice slowly getting louder and tilt my head to listen. It's coming from the left... A different cell? Probably. More enemies, or is this something else?

It goes quiet for a while, and I hang there, lifting my legs to keep the blood pumping and my heart racing to force the drugs out faster. That's when I hear the voice again. This time it's... singing?

It's loud and off-key, and there is laughter between notes.

Captivity and torture can break the mind like that. I wonder how long they have been down here. It continues though, and I snarl, getting annoyed. The high-pitched notes pierce through the bricks and hammer into my oversensitive, drugged skull.

"Shut the fuck up," I yell, and it stops instantly. There is a moment of peace before I get a response.

"Who the fuck is that? They locked you down here with me? You must be a monster. So who are you?" She laughs, her voice husky and velvety.

I stay silent, but she becomes insistent. "Who are you?" she sings, and I hear the rattle of her chains. Who did she piss off to get locked up down here?

"No one," I snarl.

"You must have a name. If you want me to shut up, you better tell me." She giggles.

Sighing, I grit my teeth. "If I tell you, you'll shut the fuck up?"

"Yup." She pops the 'p,' dragging it out.

For fuck's sake, but if it buys her silence... "Boogeyman," I tell her.

"Boogeyman, huh? Well, welcome to hell." She laughs and then goes quiet like she promised.

"This isn't hell, I've been to hell. This is nothing but an inconvenience, and I'll be free soon. Probably not you. You're better keeping your mouth shut," I growl, unsure why I'm warning her other than the wrecked, angry quality I heard in her voice. She's pissed, but she's not broken, begging, or crying. She's fucking furious.

"That won't stop them from raping and torturing me though, will it, Boogeyman? No, that will just make it easy for them, and they'll get bored and kill me. Even if every moment of my existence hurts, it's better than being dead."

I frown, wondering why. She has nothing left to fight for. She'll die down here, I've seen it so many times, and if not, she'll be broken her whole life. I don't know if it's from boredom while I wait for the people who took me or simply interest in this livid creature next to me, but I find myself asking, "Why?"

She says something that surprises me.

"For revenge."

---

## Alena

"REVENGE?" HE ECHOES IN DISBELIEF, HIS DEEP, GRAVELLY VOICE reminding me of Samuel L. Jackson.

It's soothing in a way, and I wonder what he looks like. Does he match it? Who is he? If he's locked down here like I am, he's clearly done something wrong—maybe he's one of the guards? Or just someone who pissed off the traffickers? I don't know, and he doesn't seem like the sharing type. His words are clipped, and his voice is slow and rough, like he's not used to speaking, but he's a distraction from the moral crisis brewing inside me. From the flashes of that poor innocent girl I killed. From my own pain. From the fracturing of my soul.

So I keep talking, enjoying the first real conversation I've had with someone who isn't torturing me in a long fucking time. I find myself reaching out and hanging onto his every word, not wanting it to stop.

"Yes, you know the word, Boogeyman? To get back at these bastards, to make them feel every inch of what they did to me, to rip them to pieces and fucking shower in their blood. To take everything they have and burn it to the fucking ground. That's why I'm still alive. They can take everything but that fire from me. I will get my revenge, Boogeyman, you wait and see."

He goes quiet then. I allow him the silence, since he probably doesn't know what to say. Fuck him, I don't need him. I don't need anyone. I close my eyes, shivering from the cold. The trip upstairs was a quick reprieve from the icy wetness of my cell, but the light was too bright. They are right—I'm like an animal, more suited to the cold, wet, dark cell than normal life.

I'm a creature.

The monster they created.

This place may be my prison, but it will be their casket.

---

TIME PASSES STRANGELY DOWN HERE. IT FEELS LIKE DAYS, BUT IT MUST only be an hour or so before I hear the footsteps. I've gotten good at knowing each and every sound, and those are boots headed this way. I clench my hands, my muscles tensing as I prepare for pain… which never comes.

The boots stop, and two moments later, a cell door opens. Not mine, no, my new friend, Boogeyman. I hear them enter his cell as I relax, tilting my head to try and hear better.

"Hello, Boogeyman," comes a dark voice. "I have been waiting a long time for this. It seems you are a hard ghost to track down."

"Yeah? I don't know who the fuck you are," my neighbour snaps. So this man has been hunted? Why? He clearly doesn't work for them.

"No? Maybe you'll recognise my family name, Nikolić."

There's a moment of silence, and then a bark of laughter. "You're that cunt's… brother, I'm guessing?" Boogeyman replies.

"Yes, brother. After you destroyed my family's business—"

"Of trafficking young, foreign girls," Boogeyman interrupts. There's a crash and a grunt of pain, and then the other man starts talking.

"I was all that was left. I went to America and started fresh, all while hunting you. It's taken me ten years to build contacts and regain my position, but I vowed I would never stop, no matter what it took. Even if I had to work under the directive of some fucking American scum to get to you."

"Cute backstory, can we get on with the torture now?" Boogeyman deadpans, making me laugh loudly.

"Shut that fucking dog up," comes a snarl, and there's a bang on the wall. I giggle harder, but under my breath. It seems his ten-year plan isn't going like he wanted.

I can hear the anger in his voice.

His hate.

So Boogeyman killed some traffickers, nice. It makes me wonder who the fuck he is in the first place to be mixed up with them. Either way, he's as fucked as I am. He pissed off the wrong people. This Nikolić may not be the head guy... Shit, I don't even know who the head guy is. I've only met the bald-headed fuck who runs this establishment, but he said an American? I listen harder, knowing I need to store anything they say and use it against them.

"Oh, it won't be that easy," the man snaps, and I hear another crash. "I've waited ten years, assassin, and you are going to suffer for a long fucking time down here, *сероњо*. I'm going to break every inch of your body over and over and then your will, until the big bad Boogeyman is nothing more than a fucking myth," he snarls, his Serbian accent growing more pronounced the angrier he gets.

"Pussy," Boogeyman growls. "Just like your brother."

Oh shit.

I hear the man bark something in Serbian, and then two seconds later, I hear the sound of fists hitting skin, of torture, yet Boogeyman doesn't make one sound. Not even a grunt. He just takes it, and it only infuriates them more.

I don't know how long I stand there listening to them torment him, but even I start to get angry. I don't know this man, but he clearly has balls of fucking steel and is doing the one thing I wish I could.

Pissing them off.

There's a loud yell, and a moment later, I jolt in my chains as something smashes into the wall repeatedly. I turn my head and watch as one of the bricks cracks, and pieces of it fall away, revealing a hole into the other cell. A body slides down that hole.

"Fuck, get him out of here. Leave his ass bleeding," comes a holler. "We'll be back, Boogeyman." There is a rush of footsteps, and then the sound of the cell door opening and closing.

Raising my eyebrows, I shake my head to move my hair out of my face and peer into the darkened cell next door. I get a glimpse of a giant, sweaty, bloody muscular body and chains.

"You really pissed him off." I laugh. I see the edge of his chin and mouth as he turns and notices the hole. "Welcome to the club."

# CHAPTER TEN

### Idris

Nikolić, so that's why I'm here. He's right—I killed his whole family. I thought I'd wiped that scum out. They were trading in flesh for far too long when the job landed in my lap. They had taken the wrong girl. A daughter of a rich diplomat. He hired us.

Me specifically.

I thought I killed them all, but I was wrong, and now that mistake is costing me. I won't make it again. Before I get out of here, I'll wipe out the last of that disgusting bloodline and then approach Donald about this American who is running this trafficking ring here. He can't know, can he? A ring right in his city? How could he let that happen?

Is that what Spider meant when he warned me?

Either way, it's too late now, I'm involved.

"You alive?" the woman asks.

"Yes." I don't know why I reply, even as I turn my head and spot her through the small hole. All I can see are pale, blood-streaked arms and long black hair with an eye peeking through.

"So you're an assassin, huh?" she queries. I roll my eyes and look away, not willing to talk. "That's cool as shit. I'm guessing you killed his family and now he's pissed, as in swearing vengeance standing over a grave pissed?"

"Pretty much," I snap, wanting her to know this conversation is over. I'm not a talker. Why is this bitch not getting the picture?

She goes quiet after that, thank fuck, and I close my eyes and focus on centering myself. On listening, learning, and watching. The few injuries they managed to land don't even bother me as I hang here. The hours pass slowly, creeping by, but I'm used to being patient, used to waiting and watching for my targets.

I hear the boots heading my way again and keep my eyes closed. They are back for round two it seems. I wonder how they will try to break me this time. Do they not realise I have been tortured, stabbed, shot, and blown up? Fuck, I was in a hole in the ground for days while we waited to attack a warlord's camp in Cambodia.

Nothing they can do will hurt me.

I hear the door open, followed by the sound of three pairs of feet entering the cell before they stop. I feel their eyes on me, and I slowly open mine.

Standing before me is the one person I got into this mess for, the woman who I thought was gone or dead by now.

Bessie.

And she's fucking smirking at me. She doesn't look like my cute next-door neighbour who brought me cookies. She's in tight leather pants and a see-through crop top, her long hair is curled, her face is caked in makeup, and her red lips are tilted up as she watches me. There is a coldness, a cockiness to her face now, which matches the demeanour of the two men who bracket her.

Two guards.

"Hello, neighbour," she purrs. I yank on my chain, and she laughs. "Oh no, we wouldn't want you to hurt yourself just yet." She winks as she steps closer, running a red-tipped nail down my chest. "I'm betting you have questions." She peers up at me, blinking through long eyelashes. "Poor little Boogeyman, tricked by little old me."

I grind my teeth.

It was a trap. She was working for them all along. Why didn't they make a move sooner? Unless they were waiting, integrating her into

45

my life to ensure I would come after her. I'm betting it annoyed the fuck out of her and them that I didn't make it easy. She slaps me, but I barely flinch. I'm annoyed at myself for walking into this trap, for not seeing her for what she was. How did I get so sloppy?

Fucking retirement is making me slow, too slow. It's unacceptable. I will ensure it never happens again.

"Nothing to say? Fuck, you are such an animal. You can barely even speak. Do you know how annoying it was to drag conversations out of you? To flirt with you? You're one of the most boring jobs I have ever done. The big bad Boogeyman, but you're not scary." She leans in. "Not at all. I guess the legends were wrong. You're nothing but a retired has-been. But don't worry, I still get to have my fun. My reward, you see, for playing my part so well" —she flutters her lashes at me— "for bringing him what he wanted most... and now you're ours, Boogeyman." Her guards laugh, and she smirks as she grabs my chin.

I jerk from her grip. Her touch feels slimy and disgusting, making me tug at my chains as she laughs. "You really are something to look at though, even with all those scars. I bet you would be a good fuck. What do you say? Want some fun before you die?" She leans in and presses her lips to mine, moving them against my immobile mouth as her hand slides down my chest and cups my cock. When I don't get hard, she becomes annoyed and rips her lips away as I grin at her.

"I would rather have the torture, Bessie," I snarl.

"Name's Lola," she snaps, opening her mouth to spit more venom, but she's interrupted.

"Bessie?" the woman in the next cell wheezes. "Like the fucking cow?"

"Shut the fuck up," Bessie-Lola snarls, but it only makes the woman laugh harder. They all look at the hole, not at me. I keep my eyes on them, knowing better, but my lips quirk up at her laughter. She's right, Bessie the fucking cow.

Bessie-Lola, whatever the fuck she likes to call herself, will die painfully for tricking me.

"Moo, bitch," the female manages to say through choked laughter, and even I chuckle.

"Get in there and shut her up!" Bessie screams, and her guards rush to do just that, leaving her alone with me. I lower my head, my eyes narrowed as she looks at me. She swallows nervously when she sees her death written in my gaze. Faking confidence, she lifts her chin. She knows better than to be alone in a cell with me, yet she stays, and she knows she will die.

"Don't worry, we will have our fun. For now, we will leave you to listen to your little friend's screams." She steps back, smirking as she reaches the door without taking her eyes off me. I don't even blink, watching her like the animal she accuses me of being. "It seems everyone you get close to gets hurt, doesn't it, Boogeyman?"

With that parting shot, she slams the door shut, the lock clicking into place. My anger at her, at myself, at this fucking family that won't die fills me until I lunge, yanking on my arms again. When I get free, when they make a mistake, when they lower their guard...

They will all die.

Just then, the screams of the woman next door fill the air.

# CHAPTER ELEVEN

### Alena

I cut off my scream, swallowing it back as his fist comes again, this time hitting my exposed stomach. It steals the breath from my lungs in a grunt as I swing backwards. When I can breathe again, I spit at him and wheeze out another laugh. "Bessie cow, Bessie cow of the farm…" I singsong.

"Shut her the fuck up before Lola kills us," the other snarls, and his fist is the last thing I see as it connects with my face, knocking me out.

When I wake up again, my cell is empty. I feel blood running from my nose, my stomach cramps and aches, and my breathing is laboured. Shit, did they break my ribs again?

Everything is silent, including the man next door, and as I hang there, memories begin to crowd my mind. Of roaming hands groping me, cocks ripping me open, blood running down my thighs, and the screams of the innocent woman I killed. I can't take it. He doesn't want to talk, I know that, but I don't give a fuck. I'm using him as a distraction until they kill him or I'm free. Just as I'm about to open my mouth, his deep, rumbling timbre sounds through the hole, and I turn my head to see him hunched down, trying to look at me.

"You alive?"

"Isn't that my line? Yeah, I'm alive, I've survived a lot worse," I croak, and he grunts.

"Least you're not dead, I hate the smell of rotting corpses."

"Such a poet." I grin, and he goes quiet. "That's it? That's your whole conversation? Cow Bessie is right, you're not a talker."

"Nothing to talk about," he retorts.

"No?" I fight back the memories. That's what they wanted, for me to remember I belong to them, that I'm a monster. A dog, like they call me. "What's your name?" He doesn't respond, so I try something else. "Assassin. So you kill people, right?"

He doesn't answer, and my voice lowers as the words escape without conscious thought. "Does it ever get easier?" My question drops into the silence, and I feel his gaze on me. I refuse to look away, to be ashamed. I did what I had to, but I have to know from a professional... Does this feeling ever go away? This dirty, wrong, guilty feeling?

"Why?" he retorts.

"I-I had to kill someone. They were innocent." I swallow down the pain, hating the weakness in my voice. "Does it get easier?"

"People always say no. They say it scars their soul. That they never forget their eyes or their names or the feel of the blood or the sound of the shot." He grunts and then pauses. "The truth is, I've killed so many people, they are a blur. I feel almost nothing after I pull the trigger. I'm just... empty. It wasn't easy the first time, but it wasn't hard, it just felt... right. Which in turn felt wrong. Why should it feel right to kill? But as the light left his eyes and my blade dripped with his blood, I realised I was good at it. Really fucking good." His breathing is heavier now. This wasn't what I was expecting, but for some reason, it settles me. "I'm a monster for my crimes. My soul is so black, I will burn forever. I know that, but I don't fucking care. One more body, one more death, it means nothing to me."

"Then why did you retire?" I ask, remembering the earlier conversation.

He goes silent again, and I think I pushed it too far. "It was too easy. Too fucking simple. Nothing challenged me anymore, nothing made me feel alive. During one mission, I killed an entire camp of people, and after, while I stood surrounded by bodies, ready to start clean-up, I saw a little girl, crying and screaming for her mother with a bear in her arms. Yet I felt nothing." His chains slink. "Not guilt for taking her family away, not worry, just nothing. Calm, collected. She was a loose end, but I couldn't pull the trigger, not anymore. It shouldn't be that easy." He looks at me again. "It should hurt, you should struggle. If you don't, what makes you better than them?"

"It's not heroes and villains." I laugh cruelly. "Sometimes, you have to fight evil with evil."

"Hero? I've never been a hero, little girl, so don't expect me to save you," he growls out.

I'm angry now.

"I'm not, I'll save my fucking self, asshole," I snap. "You killed. You didn't care. So what? Were the people you targeted killed for a reason? Were they bad people? One life to save hundreds and all that bullshit. I think you're lying to yourself about it. You liked the way it felt, you liked it and that scared you, so you ran." I hear him growl, and I know I've hit a nerve. "I heard your breathing, the pleasure in your voice as you spoke. You're a killer, good for you. You enjoy the work. Why is that so wrong? This world is filled with pain, death, and evil fucking bastards. They need killing. Enjoy it, 'cause they sure as shit will enjoy torturing you, assassin."

"Shut the fuck up," he snarls.

I laugh and turn away. "Better find that assassin in you again, Boogeyman, or you'll die like so many did at your hands. You won't find redemption or forgiveness here, if that's what you're thinking—there is only death. Death and pain. So why not do what you do best? Kill."

He doesn't reply.

"Looks like we aren't so different after all, Boogeyman. We were both betrayed, and now I'm betting you want revenge just as much as me. Wanna team up?" I joke.

A small, cruel smile tips up his bloody lips. I see the side of it.

'The Boogeyman and the Bitch' has a nice ring to it.

A civvie and an assassin, side by side… worlds apart. He lived in the dark, me in the light, but none of it matters down here.

Here in the shadows, there's only survival and revenge.

Vengeance is my only goal, and maybe I can use him to achieve it. He might be a killer, a murderer, but I'm what they made me.

I'm not empty like him.

I'm so full of rage and hate, it blinds me. It might even get me killed, but I'll take some of those bastards down with me if it's the last thing I do.

To kill a monster, I'll become a monster, even one bigger than the Boogeyman.

He's wrong. I don't need a hero or even a partner, I just need a weapon.

## CHAPTER TWELVE

Idris

I ignore her.
She wants to team up? Not fucking likely. I work alone. Always have, always will. I push her voice away, ignoring her derisive laughter over calling me out on my shit. She should be disgusted, horrified by what I admitted to her… yet she didn't even blink.

No, she told me to be who I am, to stop running.

Is that what I'm doing? Running? No, fuck no.

One little girl isn't going to make me question my choices. I left that life for my own reasons. I'm happy now, retired, relaxed, enjoying the simpler things… Right? Yes, it's fucking boring sometimes. Yes, I get antsy. I wake up with my hand on my gun, my heart racing and ears straining to hear enemy footsteps. So fucking what if I miss the adrenaline? If I miss the travel and excitement?

Being bored is better than being a monster.

It was always so easy for Donald to send me on the missions no one else could or wanted to do. The ones to hunt down our own, the ones where I should have died. But I never did. I was his favourite secret weapon, the monster in the shadows he warned you about, reminding you not to betray our people.

The Clergy doesn't fuck about. You want out? You pay in blood. I did that. With my own and the thousands of people I killed for them. I push away thoughts of that last mission, of the one we faked my death in. It was a shit show from start to finish, but I was free.

How the fuck did I end up right back in the middle of the game?

"So, Boogeyman, I can see your muscles, but are you hot?" she queries, her voice loud through the hole. I frown. She wants to know if I'm hot? After we just discussed me murdering people? "Just a question, don't get all growly again. Least if I die down here, I want to look at something pretty again."

When I don't respond, she laughs.

"Figured. You're like one of those gym fuck boys with all the muscles but a weird face, right? Don't worry about it, they fucked up my face too. And my body. Guess we match."

"What did they do?" I find myself asking. Why the fuck can't I stop talking to the woman? I should be planning my escape, not engaging this insane bitch.

"What didn't they do?" she retorts, her tone cruel. "At least now I don't give a fuck about hurting myself or getting fucked up while I escape and kill them. I'll probably have to become a recluse in the woods after to find peace."

"Peace is overrated," I mutter.

"Huh?"

"It's overrated," is all I say.

"What about you, Boogeyman? Planning to return to your nice, quiet life when you get free? I'm guessing you're aiming to escape, right? Mind telling me how?"

"I'm still working on it," I mumble as I look around.

She laughs harder. "Sure, let me know when you figure it out."

"I'm not taking you with me," I snarl, straining in the chains to see her. I watch her head turn, and I catch a glimpse of pale skin intersected by scars and a smirking mouth. "You will only slow me down."

"Or maybe you'll slow me down, retiree. I'm not asking us to be besties or even fucking knitting partners. I'm asking that should you get free, at least let me out so I can kill these motherfuckers. So I can split their skin down the middle and let them feel one goddamn inch of the pain they made me feel. You can walk away and never look back and return to your perfect retired life. I don't give a fuck. All I want is their screams and for them to pay."

"They all say that, then they wimp out at the first sight of blood, of death, and their screams. No one can handle it, even when they fool themselves into thinking they can. If you get free, you should go back to your nice normal life."

"You don't know me, Boogeyman," she shouts. "You don't know what they've made me do, what they did to me. I won't puke, run away, or be horrified. How could I? I've lived through worse. I don't give a fuck about settling down, getting married, and having the perfect two-point-five kids and a house anymore. I don't care about promotions or the best boring nine to five job, or even waiting around for texts from an idiot I like. That was the old me, a past fucking life. It seems so long ago. They stripped me back, tore me down, and burned that out of me. I'm nothing but an angry fucking psychopath now. I can feel the madness, the hatred leaking from me. I'll never go back to a normal life. But what I can do is make them pay. So don't you ever think you know me. Just because you've lived in darkness doesn't mean you know someone else's shadows. You'll underestimate me just like everyone else always does, just like they did, and they'll die for it. You can either help or stay the fuck out of my way."

My eyebrows rise at her conviction, even as my cock hardens from the venom in her tone, from the fight. It's not the cunt between her legs that makes me think she won't be able to do what she says, but the lack of experience. Killing isn't easy. She's done it once and seems twisted up about it. Can she really kill those who have hurt her? Or will she falter and die herself?

Why do I care?

Maybe it's the strength in her voice, the anger, the hatred I hear—it's the same that flows through me. Maybe it's just the proximity, or the fact I heard her suffering, which I saw firsthand. I know what it takes to stay alive, to keep your mind intact while being tortured. She's clearly been down here a while, and to survive what they've done to her? That takes a strength you can never learn or gain. It takes mental fortitude, something you're born with.

No, their dog, as they call her, is a lot stronger than they think. I just don't know if it will be enough to survive what's to come. She thinks what she'll do to them when she escapes will be bad...

But she has nothing on me.

Bessie-Lola, although we weren't friends or close, betrayed me. Tricked me. She'll regret that when her screams ring through my ears, and as for the last of the Nikolić bloodline... It's time that was wiped out for good.

I hear footsteps again, and the woman next to me sighs. "Want to take bets on who they're coming for, big guy?" she calls, but I just stare straight ahead. "I'm betting on me. Try not to get turned on from the bloodshed and screams. Or if you do, at least wait until they're done so I can watch you come," she jokes as I hear her door open. My eyes widen, even as my cock pulses. The idea of her watching me, of me getting off while she's hurt, is strangely arousing, even though I realise that thought's wrong.

It's sick, but when have I ever been normal?

"Hello, boys. Come to play, have we?" she taunts.

## CHAPTER THIRTEEN

Alena

They don't speak, and their faces are stern. This is a reminder, a warning to behave. I don't know if they heard us or if it's because I pissed off that cow chick, but they are here to dole out pain and suffering. To try to break me again. I tilt my head back with a smile as one steps forward, cracking his knuckles. The other, a huge Russian covered in tats, turns and watches the door. He stands with his arms crossed, leaving the tall, blond-haired skinny man to dispense the punishment.

He wastes no time getting started, not letting me taunt or tease, knowing my smart mouth is the only weapon I have. He doesn't even look directly at me, reminding me I'm nothing to them but a chore, a job.

He uses his hands first. I regulate my breathing and don't tense as he methodically punches my stomach, my sides, and my face before he breaks two of my toes and then resets them. By the time he pulls out the pliers, I know this is going to be bad.

He's a professional.

When he removes the third fingernail, I scream. It erupts out of me like a battle cry. The agony-ridden sound makes Boogeyman growl like an animal. I cut the rest off, wanting to be strong. I can't let him think I'm weak. My head hurts from the pain, but I laugh. "Don't worry, Boogeyman, we are just having some foreplay. Ain't that right, blondie?" I lift my head, and he finally meets my eyes. His are cold, ice-cold, and dead inside. There's nothing there. He doesn't speak or blink as he turns and places the pliers on the bag he rolled out before picking up a knife.

I suck in a breath and lick my chapped, torn lips.

"Do you prefer knives or guns, Boogeyman?" I ask nervously as blondie moves towards me.

"My hands," is his short, clipped reply, and my fucked-up body ignites with lust. My clit throbs with my heartbeat, which doesn't go away, even when blondie stops before me and presses the knife to my stomach. I shouldn't be turned on, I shouldn't want the assassin. Is my body really that fucked up—

*Fuck!*

The agony is sudden and sharp as he digs the long blade into the tender flesh of the only unmarred patch of skin on my body, just above my belly button. His eyes roll up to me as he drags the knife down my flesh, cutting it open. I choke back bile as he licks his lips. My breathing stutters, and my heart hammers, making the blood flow faster. He methodically wipes it away, like one would with tattoo ink, but then he lifts his bloodstained hand, and his eyes flare with something other than ice.

Desire.

I do vomit this time, all over his legs and boots. He gets mad and backhands me. A moment later, I feel the blade pressing against my skin again. Nothing is going to stop him. I close my eyes and hang there as he slices. I can't look, all I can do is breathe through the agony and try not to pass out. It feels like he's cutting me to pieces. Short, sharp strokes carve across my stomach, and then it stops as suddenly as it began. I open my eyes, unable to look down in fear of what he's done, even as he presses the bloody knife to his lips before dropping it.

His eyes are on his handiwork, not me, like I'm a piece of cattle. He frees his cock from his trousers and starts stroking it. My nose scrunches in disgust as I watch him caress it and the eight piercings running down its length. He tugs it in hard, sudden bursts. His chest heaves, and within a minute, he finds his release, his mouth opening on a silent moan, and that's when I see the old, brown stump of where his tongue used to be.

It's been burnt or cut out.

His cum splashes across my hip and leg as he wordlessly shivers before tucking his cock away. With one last look at his handiwork, he grabs his bag, rolls it up, and departs with his friend. They leave me hanging here, bleeding, as waves of burning agony wash through me. The pain becomes stronger, increasing with each breath, and I slump as tears fill my eyes.

It hurts so much that I bite my tongue, feeling blood well as I try to fight it, but it only seems to get worse as all my injuries overwhelm me. The shock is wearing off, making way for pain.

I cough before spitting some blood on the floor, then I lift my head and look through the hole. My eyes are too blurry to see, so I force my voice through my sore throat. "Did you come too?" I rasp.

He doesn't respond, and my head drops from exhaustion, even as I smile a little through the blood in my mouth.

"I bet you did. You're just as fucked up as I am. I bet you liked my screams—" The words cut off as my throat stops working.

"Don't die," is all he says, and I pass out.

When I wake up, I'm shivering, cold, and still exhausted. My head pounds and my body aches, but at least I didn't die like he ordered. I hang here, listening, but his breathing is even. Is he asleep? I doubt it. I can almost feel his eyes staring through the small hole.

Is he disgusted?

Do I care?

I shiver harder when I feel cum slowly dripping down my thigh. I must not have passed out for too long. It slithers down my leg and then drops to the floor, and for some reason, my stomach heaves. I guess you never get used to it. The horrors surge in my head, of the first time, of every time. My screams and struggles flow through my mind.

I begin to fight against my restraints, twisting my hands, trying to force my eyes open to forget, to not think about it. Otherwise, I might break. But for the first time, the pain of the cuffs cutting into my skin doesn't push it back.

I need something more, I need an anchor, so I do the only thing I can…

I reach for him.

"Tell me a story?" I whisper through the pain. He doesn't respond, and I squeeze my eyes together, hating the feeling of my dripping blood and the agony ripping through me, making me weak.

Defenceless.

Alone.

"Please, distract me. Talk to me at least?" I plead, feeling vulnerable. I hate the quiver in my voice. I hate that I'm reaching out to this stranger and asking him. But there is nothing like shared trauma and torture to bring strangers closer… right?

He doesn't respond, and my tears fall. I think he's going to let me suffer, but then his voice rings out hesitantly. "When I'm free, I'll start at the bottom with the bodyguards. They won't stand a chance. I'll kill them quickly. Once they are out of the way, I'll hunt down the handlers. They will suffer more. After they are dead, I will find those who run this operation. Each person who bought from them, each silent investor or person who looked the other way. And then those who are the shadow partners."

Step by step, he tells me how he's going to kill them. From breaking bones and ripping out throats, to slowly dissecting organs and filleting skin. He gives me each excruciating, painful detail. His voice starts calm, but as he goes on, it gets deeper, gravellier, and his breathing picks up a bit. I find my heart racing, my own breathing matching his as something akin to… to desire flares within me.

Not just for him, but for his words. For the pain he's promising.

I want that. I want the beautiful agony he's voicing.

The oblivion, the assurance of vengeance.

He may be a monster, but for some reason, I like that. My body does too. I don't know if it's the strength there, the darkness and bloodlust, but I feel something for this killer—a low fire igniting in my already aching stomach.

I want to watch the blood run across him, across us both. My pussy clenches as I imagine him killing them in front of me and offering me their heads, their hearts, as he cuts them to pieces like they did me.

I'm going to fuck Boogeyman, and then I'm going to hunt with him.

He just doesn't know it yet.

---

THEY LEAVE ME THERE ALL NIGHT AND MOST OF THE NEXT DAY. I speak to Boogeyman, telling him random shit to keep my mind off my stomach. I won't even look at it, knowing somehow, deep down, it will cut that last thread of humanity I have left.

It's bad, I know it.

He doesn't always respond, but he listens. I see him through the hole. He even smirks when I tell him tales or random shit that comes into my mind. I'm so busy spinning a story about breaking a boy's nose as a kid that I don't hear them until it's too late.

My door is ripped open, and the man standing there smirks. Bessie is behind him, how lovely. "Get the dog." She grins. "Let's toss her to the assassin and let him have some fun with her."

The guard grins at me. He's a usual visitor to my cell. Fuck. "Can I have some fun with her first? She tastes so sweet." I almost gag. The fucking sick bastard likes to drink my blood. One time when I had my period, they just let it drip down my legs and beat me for it, calling me dirty and disgusting… but him? He drank it down while I cried and screamed.

He likes my blood? I'll make him choke on it when I'm free.

"Fine," Bessie snaps, and then she grins as she looks me over. "Why not play with her in front of him and let him see what happens to those we don't like? Show him something he can't stop. He has a soft spot for women and innocents. Make him angry." She laughs and walks away as he smiles and steps closer.

"Hear that, dog? We get to have some fun."

"Amazing," I rasp and then tense, flicking my eyes around. They are going to unchain me and put us in the same cell. This is my chance.

They think they are torturing us, but instead, they are giving me what I wanted... and him?

They are providing him with an opportunity to escape.

He unlocks my cuffs, and I drop to the floor. My arms and legs are dead, and my stomach pulses in pain along with my fingers and toes. I groan, my face pressed to the wet floor as I scrabble at the stone. He laughs and kicks me, and I roll across the floor from the force. I hit the back wall, and something sharp stabs into my palm. My eyes fly open. Sticking out from the rock is a bent, rusted piece of metal. I've never been this far into the cell, tied up as I was.

My back is to the room, so he can't see what I've found. I grab it and begin to pull with my blood-soaked fingers, but they slip and I cut myself, hissing as I hear him moving closer. I don't have long, but I need to get it free and fast. It's my only weapon. Maybe I can use it to escape.

It's better than nothing.

"Get up, dog," he barks. "Hiding won't stop this." He laughs, but I ignore him and grit my teeth, disregarding the pain from my ruined fingers to grip the rusted metal, twist, and yank it. My heart slams as he gets closer. When he's above me, I curl around it so he can't see what I'm doing, pretending like I'm crying or hiding. He kicks me softly, teasingly, as he laughs. I pull and pull, and when he reaches down and grabs me, throwing me across the space, the metal comes with me.

I roll, and when I stop, I conceal it in my palm, clenching my fingers around it like I'm creating a fist with both hands. Victory! I almost grin before closing my eyes and feigning agony, going limp. He picks me up and tosses me over his shoulder and leaves my cell.

He takes me where I want to be—with the assassin. The door opens, then there are footsteps, and another door opens as the guard who was waiting outside the cell speaks. "I'll go wait at the end. Have your fun, but don't be too long," he orders, and the door shuts behind us once more. I crack open my eyes and get my first look at the assassin. My breath catches in my throat at the beauty and power of the chained man.

His arms are extended above him, and his feet barely touch the floor. Muscles upon muscles are corded across his body. He's a weapon, wielding such strength, such power. His head lifts, and his dark eyes lock on me. They're filled with something, a darkness, a fire, and such strength, it stops my heart. His full lips are flat, his chiselled cheeks are clenched, and his strong jaw is sharp enough to cut glass. His neck strains, causing his veins to pop.

He looks like a demon, a chained Lucifer. He's calm, collected, and in control, even chained like an animal.

He's not just good-looking, he's breathtaking.

Covered in scars, he will never be traditionally attractive, but each raised, bevelled line intersecting across his tanned skin only makes me stare harder. We match. His thick thighs are encased in jeans, which are covered in blood, and his long limbs lead to bare, bloody, huge feet. He's a fucking giant. Big everywhere. Enormous, actually.

I've never seen a man like him in real life. In porn and films sure, but before my own eyes? Never. He's what poets talk about, what Greek gods were based on. He's a being to be reckoned with, but it's more than the scars, the body, and the dark and dangerous vibe pumping through him that stills me.

It's those eyes.

I know why they fear him. In those depths, I see such death, such need for violence, it awakens my desire again. I could lose myself forever in his darkness, and I would die with a smile on my face with those hands wrapped around my neck as he snaps it.

He's a killer, a murderer. Even though he already told me, I can see it in his gaze and in the anger coating him like a second skin.

My ogling is cut short as I'm dropped to the floor. "Ready to have some fun for our audience, dog?" The guard grins down at me as I hide my hand by my side, staring up at him from my back, the wind knocked out of me. "Don't worry, assassin, I'll leave what's left of her for you. We know you like to rip them up."

Boogeyman growls, "Don't."

The guard ignores him, kneeling on either side of my hips as he grins, his hard cock pressed against his trousers. His hands dart out and wrap around my neck. He likes to choke me until I almost die, then fuck me while I struggle to breathe. He likes my pain, my blood, but it seems he wants this to last so he can put on a show like he said.

He isn't playing. He squeezes hard. I feel my eyes bug out as I scratch his hand with my empty one, half fighting. I need to, or he'll wonder what's going on. I kick and twist as he laughs, faking it even as I grip the metal shard tighter.

A plan comes to mind.

My revenge starts here while Boogeyman watches.

## CHAPTER FOURTEEN

Idris

I struggle and lunge in my chains as I roar, trying to get to her as he chokes her. When I see one of her hands slowly rise, I still, staring in confusion. He doesn't notice, he's too busy laughing as he watches the light leave her eyes.

Even as she dies, she fights. My heart slams as I watch. Her eyes dart to me for a second before they lock back on the man above her, and with more strength than I thought she had left, she stabs him with something too quickly for me to catch. He screams and falls back with a piece of metal sticking from his eyeball. Blood pours down his face as he howls.

She coughs and sucks in air but doesn't wait. Stumbling to her feet, she jumps at him and knocks him to the floor. He tries to slap her away, but he's weak from shock. She grabs the metal and stabs his face and chest repeatedly, screaming. Her body is covered in wounds and blood, hers and his as it flies through the air. She stabs over and over until she can't anymore.

She slumps slightly, breathing heavily as the man screams and bucks beneath her.

"You like blood, asshole? Choke on yours," she snarls, and then with one more downward stroke, she impales the metal into his neck.

Deep.

Blood instantly sprays and pumps around it, and just like she said, he starts to choke. Eyes wide, he slaps at it with his hands, trying to cover it as it bubbles on his lips. He sputters, blood spotting his face and hers. She observes, her hips moving softly at first before she speeds up.

She's rubbing herself against him as she watches him die.

When he stops moving or making a noise, and his hands drop to the sides, she falls backwards. She lies on her back with a smile on her lips while her eyes lock on the ceiling, her body pale.

I've seen glimpses of her through the hole, but seeing her in her full glory, in her beauty, pain, and rage... my cock hardens. She's incredible. She has long black hair that's jagged on one side, cut shorter like a diagonal line, giving her a dangerous look. Her dark, deep eyes have amber flecks, and they spit fire at everyone she looks at. She is tall, and I can tell she used to be curvy, with big, wide hips and thick thighs with long lean legs. She has large perky breasts and an ass for days with adorable dimples and tiger stripes across it. Her pale skin is coated in blood, and her face is stunning, with arched eyebrows, plush bloody lips, and a long regal nose.

She's beautiful, even more so covered in scars and blood. She looks like a fighter, like what I imagined Amazon warriors looked like—fierce and unafraid. Each scar only adds to her appeal, and I run my tongue along my teeth as I trace my eyes over her nude body, aching to feel every dip and raised line.

*Desire.*

It's been a long time since I've felt lust for anything other than death. Women just didn't put up a good enough fight to distract me from my own brain, so I gave up. But this creature, fuck. My cock is throbbing, leaking. I can feel it, despite the situation we are in... or maybe in reaction to it. Her chest heaves, her perky rose coloured nipples are pebbled, and her belly is quivering, though it's covered in blood with a fresh carving that has anger flowing through me at someone marking her up like this.

They called her a dog, but didn't they see this magnificent creature is no fucking animal? She's indescribable. My hands ache to grip her, hold her, as I shove into that cunt I can almost smell. To feel her beneath me or above me. For her to ride me. To feel her heat, her blood, and the throb of her racing pulse as I hold her life in my hands.

I'd probably kill her, but wouldn't it be fucking wonderful?

She's just lying there, and I run my gaze over her thighs, her tits, and her face. We need to get out of here. She wants freedom? She wants to kill them? So do I. Maybe I'll let her tag along for entertainment, to see that again, and then I'll fuck her over their corpses and leave her there.

"Finished?" I ask, and she rolls her head to look at me and grins.

"Who's weak now, bitch?" She grins and then starts to sit up, but she winces and looks down. She freezes then. Is it the first time she's seen it? That strong, slightly crazy woman fades, and in her place is a hurt, wounded animal.

She snaps.

I frown as she gets up and leaps at the dead man, hitting and kicking him. Sighing, I look around before addressing her. "Bring me his keys," I demand, but she ignores me, screaming like she's feral, even as she rips her cuts and causes more blood to pour down her frame. "Stop," I snarl, my voice loud and severe. She does after a few more blows and then lifts her head, her hair blocking her face as she peers at me. "Get over here now," I order, my eyes narrowed.

She throws her hair back and stands on wobbly feet before moving over to me. She stops in front of me and meets my eyes, and in hers, I see fear and hatred, and then she looks down at her stomach again.

"He carved his name into me," she whispers brokenly. I hate it.

"Where the fuck is that strong bitch?" I snap. "So fucking what? Don't you stand there fucking crying, that's weak girl shit. You want out? You want revenge? Get the fucking keys."

Her head snaps up, and she lunges at me, punching me over and over, but I just take it. Her hits are strong but not strong enough. When she steps back, panting, I raise my eyebrows. "You'll pay for that, little one. Now get the keys before I rip these chains free, wrap them around your neck, and strangle the life out of you for wasting time."

She looks back down at her stomach, not hearing me. I snarl, losing my temper. We don't have time for this. It's clear the rough, crudely carved name on her stomach is throwing her though. She's lost in her mind, in her pain. This one last act of defiance is fading from her. Maybe she isn't as strong as I thought.

"Stupid bitch," I mutter.

She screams at me before turning and grabbing the keys. Ignoring me, she gets on her tiptoes and reaches for one of the cuffs, grunting when the movement pulls on her still bleeding belly, and frees one hand before tossing the keys at me. I catch them, rotating my wirst to restore blood flow. Eyes on her, I undo the other cuff and step forward. I do some stretching to restore blood circulation before I stare at her once more.

"We need to do something about that, or you will be useless to me." I nod at her stomach. "You choose. Either I burn it or change it."

"What?" She steps back, retreating. I follow, cornering her against the wall, and then I place my arm above her head as I glare down at her.

"It's stopping you. I need it to fuel you. If you can't look at it or are going to break when you think about it, we need to change it before we move on. You want revenge?" I ask, and she nods, her mouth thinning in anger. I lean down and rub my thumb across her tempting bloody lips. "Then stop being a weak, broken victim. Be that bitch who defied them, who faced me down and didn't even blink, or I'll leave you here with them to rot like the weak dog they think you are."

I step back. It's her choice. I don't know why I'm offering her one, I should leave her.

But she interests me, plus she may come in handy.

"What's your choice?" I demand.

## CHAPTER FIFTEEN

### Alena

My breath freezes as I stare into those dark, dangerous eyes. He means it. I have a choice, it's my body, but if I choose wrong, he will leave me here without a thought. He's built like that. He said he wasn't a hero, and he truly meant it. He would leave me here to die without a backwards glance. If I want my revenge, I first need to rectify what they did to me. For some reason, the carving in my stomach is breaking me like nothing else has.

I need it to be gone, which isn't an option. But I can change it. I can stop it from being my weakness and make it my strength.

I have an idea.

Turning away, I crouch down, spurred by the pain as it pulls on the letters carved into my skin. I search the dead guard's pockets until I find his sharp, glinting knife, and then I stand and turn to Boogeyman. He frowns in confusion as I pull the knife out and show it to him. His eyebrows rise, but he doesn't seem concerned I'll use it on him, so just to test him, I rush him. He snarls, grabs my throat, and slams me into the wall effortlessly, holding me above the floor as my feet kick.

His scowling face gets right into mine as he slides me up the wall with just one hand until I'm the same height as him, and then he squeezes, his lips tilted down angrily. "Don't try that shit, you'll die before you hit the floor."

I grin, even as he clenches harder. "I had to see if you were worth the hype," I wheeze, and press the blade to his chest. "Here, I don't have a steady enough hand." I cough, and he releases his grip enough so I can talk. My body lights up at almost being pressed against his. My needy, idiot pussy pulses unashamedly at the strength he has in just one hand. "You'll have to do it."

"Do what?" he asks, even more perplexed.

"Change it, carve it into something else," I rasp and then relax into his touch, smiling at him. "I won't even fight you... or I'll try not to." He smirks. "I'm not saying I won't swear or scream…"

"Oh, don't worry, it won't stop me." He lets me go, and I slump down the wall, almost falling as he flips the blade in a quick, deft hand and balances it on one fingertip, testing it. Blood wells, and he nods before flipping it back and addressing me.

"You will probably need to lie down or you'll fall," he suggests.

"Just do it," I almost yell. There's no point in wasting time. I brace myself against the wall, keeping my eyes on his. He doesn't hesitate. He holds my waist, his hand spanning nearly all of my ribcage as he presses the blade to the wounds, not asking what to change it to. Good, I wouldn't know, but anything is better than that name on my skin. It makes me feel more violated than I've ever been before.

"It's going to hurt. Don't scream too loudly or they will come, and I'll have to stop and kill them then start again," he murmurs, and without warning, he slashes downwards. Agony roars through me, more than ever before.

I almost bite my tongue off to hold back the scream, but it slips free and he snarls, glaring at me for a moment. I heave in breaths and close my eyes as my body shakes. I pant and breathe through the sickness and dizziness, and when I feel better, I open my eyes and nod for him to continue. I brace again as he looks down, pressing the knife to my skin. The cool metal feels cold against my overheated flesh.

He cuts again, and I rip myself away with a scream. He snarls, angry now, and covers my mouth with his bloody hand, the knife still in his grasp. I taste my blood on his skin, the blade cutting into my cheek as I shake my head. He removes his hand slightly, and I wet my lips, accidentally licking away the blood. He groans as he follows the movement of my tongue with those dark, dangerous eyes. "I can't, it hurts too badly." I hate myself for admitting that.

He sighs and looks down at my stomach for a moment. "Distract me," I suggest, knowing we need to do this. He needs to finish it. I don't want to die here with my captor's name on my stomach. I can't. I won't.

"Distract me," I repeat. He meets my gaze, probably thinking I want him to talk to me, but I have something else in mind.

How do you counter pain?

Pleasure.

"Make me come," I say unashamedly as I swallow my blood. His eyes flare with interest, but he doesn't move or speak. "I'm not asking to marry you, for God's sake, I'm telling you to fuck me. Make me come while you cut me, that way I won't feel it as badly."

He doesn't move, and I snap, kicking out at him. "Fucking hell, I'll do it myself." I reach down, ignoring the feeling of my skin. The last time I came, I touched myself. I didn't have this many scars, nor was I this skinny. He holds my gaze as I part my thighs, grounding me to him as I rub my throbbing clit. He groans, dropping his eyes to my fingers as his muscles clench. But it's not enough, I need more... I need to feel something other than my rapists' cocks, more than my own fingers.

I need someone to take control, to bring me pleasure and not let up until I'm screaming and writhing. I whimper, rubbing desperately before gliding my fingers down my pussy and dipping them inside my channel, coating them in my cream as I fuck myself on them, watching his body and eyes the entire time.

"Stop," he mutters, even as he presses closer, his dark eyes on my fingers.

"Please," I whimper.

I don't even see him move. One second, my fingers are spearing my pussy, and the next, he has them trapped in his grip between us, the glistening tips held there. My heart stutters before it races, and my nipples tighten at the raw hunger spread across that dark, dangerous face.

Eyes locked on mine, he leans in and wraps his thick lips around the tips of my fingers, the wet cavern of his mouth making me gasp. He sucks hard, and I jerk forward before he releases me and his long tongue laves my digits, cleaning them of my cream. He watches me the whole time, and when he leans back, his eyes are blown wide, his lips are parted on a groan, his cheeks are flushed, and his chest is heaving.

"Fuck," he snaps. He throws my hand away before grabbing and lifting me, and then he slams me back into the hard wall, knocking the wind from my lungs. Every man I was with before… before this shit show doesn't hold a flame to him, to the dominance and danger flowing through his veins. I've had rough sex before, but even then, they worried about hurting me, ensuring I was in the moment and okay.

Boogeyman?

He doesn't give a fuck if I'm hurt or dying. He takes what he wants, and right now, that's me. His large hands grab my thighs, the knife pressing into one of my scars and almost reopening it. The flash of pain makes me groan and rub against him. He holds me still as he lowers his head, his lips almost pressing to mine as he speaks.

"I won't fit yet," he mutters.

"I don't care," I murmur. "Make it hurt, rip me, I don't care. Just fuck me," I snarl, fighting his hold and feeling the pain bloom in my stomach. I remember the other men's hands, their touches, their bodies. I need him to replace them with someone I choose, someone I want. "Make me bleed, make me come and scream, Boogeyman. Kill me if you can," I dare, knowing he won't back down now.

He can't.

I'm his new prey.

He lets go of one of my legs and holds me there like I weigh nothing as he reaches between us, unzips his jeans, and pulls out his hard cock. I swallow, eyes wide. Shit, he wasn't messing around. It's fucking huge, wide as hell, and so long, my eyes water at the thought of having it inside me. But under that sudden fear at the size of his monster cock is desire—a low, burning desire to feel it tear me apart, to slam inside of me as he cuts me.

To make me bleed, even as he makes me come.

I'm fucked up. I blame them. But maybe I was before I was ever kidnapped. I don't give a fuck, it's not going to change now. This is who I am, and I refuse to be ashamed or hate myself the way they want me to. My body has got me through all the torture and trauma, and now it gets what it wants.

Boogeyman... Shit, I can't keep calling him that.

"What's your name?" I ask, my eyes flickering to his then back down to his monster cock.

He ignores me, as usual.

He releases his cock and drags his open hand down my pussy, gathering my cream before wrapping it around his hard length and stroking, coating it in my need. I shiver in his hold, watching him. My breathing quickens as I prepare for the pain and pleasure that is soon to follow. He observes me silently the entire time.

He reaches down and slides those huge fingers, intersected with scars, down my pussy and back up before slapping my clit, making me cry out at the sudden surge of pleasure. He does it again, harder and harder, until I'm groaning and grinding into his hand, and then he moves away before circling my dripping hole.

Without warning, he shoves two of those thick, scarred fingers inside me, and the sudden, sharp pain has a squeal leaving my lips. He glares at me, silencing me as he slams them into my channel and twists, stretching me before crooking them and rubbing my wall. He brushes over that spot that has my leg jerking in his grip and my eyes closing as I relax into the wall, lifting my hips to take his fingers, even as the pain fades to a burning pleasure. He adds another and another. There are four fingers inside me, and he doesn't wait for me to adjust.

No, Boogeyman pulls them out and slams them back in, fucking me with them. The pain and pleasure mingle, making me pant and grunt as I ride them unashamedly. I shake my head, it's too much yet not enough at the same time. The wet squelch of his fingers is loud, even over my breathing, as he rams them into me.

He's finally had enough, silencing my cries by smashing his lips against mine. I moan into his mouth as he forces my lips open and slips his tongue in, tangling it with mine. He dominates my mouth as his hand speeds up, his thumb hitting my clit in sync with his thrusts. I lift and grind, twisting on his hand as he swallows my cries. I have to rip my head away, needing to breathe, and he kisses down my chin to my chest. His tongue drags through the blood there as he rolls his eyes up to watch me.

He blows air over my hard nipple before lapping it with his tongue and finally drawing it into his mouth, sucking hard before his teeth come down on the tip. He bites into my sensitive skin until I cry out again. Growling in anger, he slips his fingers from my channel for a moment as he juggles me, and then I feel something cold and wet against my clit and pussy.

Hard.

Metal.

The knife.

He pops my nipple from his mouth. "Scream one more time, and I'll cut your clit, understood?" he snarls. My eyes widen as my pussy clenches, and I nod. His head lowers again, going to my other breast, leaving a bite mark behind. His fingers pummel into my pussy, restarting that punishing pace as he builds me higher and higher towards an orgasm. I don't know if it's him, the pain, or the threat of the knife, but it has me wilder than ever.

I twist and buck, biting my lip to stop myself from crying out. I fight him... and Boogeyman? He loves it. He eats it up. He slams me against the wall, removing his hand just as I was about to fall into the abyss of an orgasm. I feel his cock then, pressing to my pussy as he releases my nipple and leans back, staring at me. His lips are red, and his eyes are wild. He pushes the knife harder against my clit, grinding it down, and it throws me over the edge.

I come so hard I see stars.

Yet through that pleasure, I feel the knife move, and a moment later, agony tears through me. I force my eyes open, even as my legs shake and my pussy pulses. The pain and pleasure meet, making me silent and wild. Blood streams down my belly to my pussy, mixing with my cream.

He cuts me as I come. He makes another quick slice and then pushes his cock into me, forcing it through my tight, fluttering channel with a snarl. He pulls out and pushes back in, even as I struggle to breathe, caught in his grip like a bunny in a net.

Nothing compares to him. I thought I was strong. So strong, so sure. Boogeyman is a monster. He craves pain, bloodshed, and chaos, and he's fucking me, forcing that huge cock into my pussy and not giving me an inch of leeway. The knife is still pressed against my skin, waiting for the next cut. The anticipation makes me gasp as I look down, watching his huge cock stretch my hole as it rams in and out of me, glistening with my cream and blood.

As I'm looking, he takes the knife and rubs the blunt side against my clit. The pleasure builds again, mixed with pain and fullness, and I'm on the cliff, coming again when he runs the wet knife across my skin to the side, digging the sharp end into one of the healing letters. With a smooth move, he swipes down.

My head falls back as I fight through the haze of pain that slowly tips to pleasure as he fucks me with long, hard thrusts, slanting my hips to hit that spot inside me over and over again. My eyes close without permission, my body tightens up, and every single part of me hurts and sparks with pleasure. I can't breathe.

Can't see.

Can't think or hear.

All I feel is the mixture he's created as the pleasure grows, tempered each time he slices.

He brings the handle of the knife to my clit as he fucks me, throwing me back over that edge again and making me come. He leans in and swallows my scream, my blood undoubtedly rubbing across his body as I squirt around his cock.

He groans into my mouth, slamming into me and stilling. I feel his cum filling me. His tongue and cock anchor me to this world when I feel like I might fall into the abyss of darkness. The pain, the pleasure are too much, but he keeps me here, dragging me back until I feel every hard, hurting inch of it.

When I can finally pry my eyes open again, they lock on his dark ones. He's breathing heavily too, and I can hear the racing of his heart as he pins me to the wall, his softening cock still inside me. Without a word, he pulls out and drops me to my feet. I slide down the wall to my ass, wincing at the pain it causes in my sore pussy and stomach.

He licks his lips, buttoning his jeans as I watch. His stomach is coated in my blood, and for some reason, that makes my breath catch, seeing those glistening abs move and the bright crimson marking him. Swallowing, I drag my gaze away and drop them to my stomach to see what he did.

He's changed the letters. They are bloody and red, contrasting with my pale stomach like a declaration.

"Bitch?" I read, then lift my head to see him smirking at me.

At least it isn't 'dog' or some shit. In fact, I kinda like it.

"That's my name now?" I ask.

"Yes, now get your ass up. It's time to get your revenge, Bitch."

## CHAPTER SIXTEEN

Idris

She stands as I turn away, breathing through the pleasure still roaring through me like a tidal wave. Watching her scream, fight, and bleed while I fucked that tight wet cunt... Shit. A man could become addicted.

*Focus.*

I ignore the sound of her moving around, even though I seem to be attuned to her. Crouching, I search the dead guard. He doesn't have keys for the door, and his boots are way too small. I do take the shard of metal though and thrust it at her. "Here," I murmur, and then stomp to the door and bang on it.

Nothing happens, so I do it again.

Louder.

I hear footsteps then and slide to the right where the door will swing open. I wink at her as she stands there, naked and covered in blood, with the weapon held tightly in her hand. When it unlocks and the guard steps in, I move. He's too busy gawking at her and the dead body to notice the empty chains. His headphones hang from his neck, explaining why he didn't come faster.

I grab his neck and snap it, killing him faster than he deserves, but oh well. I let him drop with a thud and snatch the keys and tuck them into my pocket. I take his gun and knife and hold them in one hand before stripping off his shirt and tossing it at her. "Here, put that on," I mutter as I lean my head out and check the corridor.

It has doors all along it, metal barred ones like the one we're in. They are all open apart from mine and hers though. To the right, at the end of the corridor, is a locked and chained metal gate, and beyond that is a small set of stairs leading to another metal door. I see no cameras or motion detectors, so I lean back in. I shouldn't have killed him. I should have tortured him and found out information on the complex, but I can find another to get it from. I was sloppy.

Maybe I was trying to show off a little, and as she finishes buttoning the long-sleeved white button-up shirt, I know it worked. She doesn't bother with the top three buttons, displaying her cleavage and scars as the shirt hangs loosely around her, stopping at the tops of her thighs. The material sticks to her stomach slightly, and her blood is starting to stain it, but she doesn't care as she steps over the body. Tossing her shaggy hair behind her and pressing herself to my side, she peeks around me before looking up.

"Well then, Boogeyman, assassins first," she teases.

Shaking my head, I check the gun before handing her the knife. She discards her metal shard and palms it, ready to go. I put the gun in the back of my jeans with the safety on for now. I won't use it unless I have to, it's too noisy. It will draw too much attention, and we want to be sneaky and silent, killing them as we go so the bosses don't try to escape.

"Don't make a sound. Do what I say, or I'll lock you back up," I order, my eyes narrowed. She rolls hers, and I swipe my hand out, wrapping it around her throat and squeezing in warning. She moans, her eyes widening in pleasure, and her lips part as she leans farther into me. "Understood?"

She nods in my grasp as I feel her heartbeat race, feel the fragility of her neck. How easy it would be to snap it. Her eyes flare like she can read my thoughts, and she relaxes into my hold, letting me choose. I release her, and she laughs, stretching up to run her lips along mine.

"Better leave some for me to kill," she purrs, and then kisses me before stepping back.

I swallow, ignoring the warmth of her touch, and turn away so she doesn't see the confusion on my face. Switching from her to work mode, I leave the room with her following me, heading straight down the corridor to the gate. Grabbing the keys, I unlock it and swing it open with a metal whine, the only sound in the silence.

I step through, having to duck, and then I carefully and noiselessly move up the steps to the door. I press my ear against it and listen, but it's too thick for me to hear anything. Sighing, I unlock it and, hand on the handle, I edge it open a crack to see out. The light out there is bright, another hallway. I hear no one, so I open it farther and look out.

There is a camera at the end of the hallway, an old-style one that turns. I count it as it rotates back to us, and I shut the door. Ten seconds. Thirty steps to the opposite end of the hallway. Easy enough.

I turn to tell her when I hear a cough and footsteps. I have an idea, so I wait, counting the steps, and when I think they are outside, I slam the door right into them. They grunt. "What the fuck, man?" the guard yells before I grab him and yank him inside, shutting the door as the camera hits our location. His eyes widen as he fumbles for his gun. I cover his mouth and wait for a response, but none comes.

Bitch slaps his hand away and grabs the gun, tutting. "Don't be rude," she scolds him. Before I can speak, she fires questions at him, questions I was about to ask, leaving me with raised eyebrows as I stare down at her. Maybe she isn't hopeless after all. "How many guards are on shift? Where are they? What are their rotations, and where are the fucking bosses?"

"Where is Lola?" I add, and she winks at me before looking back at the wide-eyed man. "I'm going to lift my hand. If you scream or say anything other than answers, I will hurt you," I warn, and I slowly peel my hand away.

"Fuck you, dog—"

I gut punch him, and he gasps for breath as I grab his head in a vice-like grip and punch him over and over until he cries out, and then I stop, noticing the pain in his eyes.

I need him awake and aware enough to answer, but also scared enough to not insult her again, or it will be his death. For some reason, it angers me that he dares to even look at her, never mind talk about her like that. She has survived too much to be disrespected. She's a warrior, like me.

When I look over at her, she's watching me with her bottom lip caught in her teeth. I run my gaze down her form, noticing her shirt is plastered to her belly now, which is bleeding freely. I need to clean it at some point so it doesn't get infected. Turning back, I lock eyes with the guard. "Let's try this again. Answer us, or I'm going to start cutting parts of you off."

I lift my hand. He swallows nervously and glances at her again, so I step closer, blocking his view. "Don't look at her. How many guards?"

"I don't know," he hedges, so I grab her knife and slice. I cut off his right ear. He screams, but I clamp my hand over his mouth, shoving his ear into it as he gags and chokes. Tears stream down his face, blood drips down his neck, and he passes out. Sighing, I let him go, watching him drop to the floor as piss covers the front of his trousers.

"Pussy." She laughs.

I grin over at her, and she crouches down and slaps him over and over again. "Hey, asshole, wake up or I'm going to let him keep cutting while you're out... In fact, let's start with your cock." He wakes up with a gasp, and she jerks back as he goes to grab her, laughing. I roll my eyes and lift him to his feet.

"One last chance, or I let her loose on you," I warn as he spits his ear onto the floor. The bloody reminder is a stark threat, which makes him pale and gag before he turns and looks over at her. She's grinning at him, swinging the gun in her hand.

"Twenty guards upstairs, ten girls are still here. The rest have gone to sale. Boss isn't here... He's in the city with Lola. It's just us guards," he rushes out.

"Cameras?" I snap.

"The command center a floor up. Take the left when you go out, and it's the room upstairs. The whole second floor is for the men."

"Where are the women?" she asks.

"This floor, locked in rooms. Please, I told you everything," he whines, and I step back.

"He's yours, Bitch," I offer, knowing from his look at her earlier that he's hurt her before. She laughs, grabs her knife, and steps up to him.

"I remember you like knives, don't you?" she murmurs and lifts her shirt. "In fact, this is your mark right here, isn't it?" She taps an older scar and then runs the knife to her mound. I press against her back as my cock hardens. "You even cut me here, didn't you? You did. I remember because I peed on you and you laughed."

He swallows, shaking his head as he cries, and she leans in. "You did. Let's match, shall we?" In one smooth move, she stabs his crotch. The man screams so I punch him, knocking him out. He falls, blood pooling around him, while she watches with rapt fascination. Placing my hands on her hips, I lift her and step back, turning her until her eyes meet mine. Her gaze is filled with desire.

"He's gone. He said twenty guards. You ready? I won't be able to protect you," I warn. Unknowingly, I reach out and cup her cheek. She leans into it with a wicked grin.

"I don't need you to," she murmurs. "I'll keep this gun and use you as a shield," she teases.

Smirking, I lean down and almost press my lips to hers. "Shoot straight and kill them all," I murmur, and then kiss her quickly, allowing myself that small pleasure before turning, gun in hand, and opening the door to see where the camera is facing.

"You know it." I hear a click and feel her breath across my arm. "Let's do this."

*Let's.*

# CHAPTER SEVENTEEN

### Alena

I'm pressed against him, using his warmth and height to make me feel secure and safe before going out there into the unknown. I don't know why he makes me feel protected. He shouldn't, he's a murderer, an assassin. He already said he will leave me, kill me. Just because he fucks like a god doesn't change that, even though he made me see stars...

Even though he hurt the guard for insulting me and lifted me so the blood didn't touch me.

*Shit, why is that so hot?*

He slips out, and I drag my head from the gutter and focus on my mission. I've been planning this for so long. He doesn't get to distract me with his cock and body. No, this is my time.

For revenge.

I follow him out. He turns left, moving quickly down the corridor. I almost have to run to keep up with my shorter legs, and when he stops at the corner, I bump into him. He grabs me to stop me from falling as he peers around the bend, and then he moves around it, dragging me after him to avoid the camera so they won't know we're coming. Boogeyman is sure and confident, knowing exactly what to do. If I

81

didn't know he was a hunter, an assassin, I would be worried about the confident, almost cocky edge to him. Like he's walking down a beach, having a nice stroll.

It's hot.

He takes the door the guard told us to, and I shut it behind us, watching him take the steps two at a time. It curves halfway up, and he stops and glances back at me with his finger on his lips. I hear talking and laughter then, even some low music. I nod, wondering how he heard it so quickly as he crouches and peeks around the corner. I stay there, observing as he glides up the stairs, and when he comes back, I move closer and he leans down. With his mouth against my ear, he murmurs, "At least fifteen there. That means some are wandering about and they will hear us. No way to go in quiet. Are you ready?"

"Yes," I whisper in understanding. He pulls back, giving me one last fierce look before pulling his gun, releasing the safety, holding it with two hands, and rounding the corner again. This time, I follow him. I have a gun and a knife. I've only shot a gun a few times with my dad when I was younger, but I remember how to hold it and aim, so it will have to do.

He doesn't creep up the stairs this time, no, he storms up them, and as soon as he reaches the top, he begins firing. He holds the gun steady as he walks, effortlessly shooting and twisting and aiming in a blink. The shots are loud, the chaos even louder. Scrambling feet, bodies dropping, yells, and crashing furniture is all I can hear between shots.

I follow after him, and I see a man fall. The hand that had been reaching for his gun now lies on the floor, lifeless. I take aim, breathe out, and squeeze the trigger. I hit a man trying to duck behind a table and grin as I follow in Boogeyman's wake. His gun clicks empty, and he drops it to the ground, rushing another who's firing. Boogeyman punches him in the throat before turning and grabbing the arm of another guard, twisting his knife around and embedding it in his chest. I watch as he swings it down again and again before dropping the man and moving on.

Then I have to concentrate on myself, because two men have noticed me and decided I'm an easier target than the big bastard currently using a silver tray to decapitate someone. One lunges for me, and I duck his punch, kicking out, but I miss, and he grabs my leg and twists me into him. He wraps his arm around my neck as I buck and hiss.

"Hey, asshole, we have your dog!" he calls.

Boogeyman stabs once more with the tray, crouching over the body before looking up, his face covered in blood splatter. He picks up a gun, and without a word, he raises it. The man holding me doesn't even have time to open his mouth before the bullet hits him in the middle of the forehead and knocks him back, the force freeing me. Boogeyman turns away and carries on shooting. Me? I dive and roll across the floor, coming up at the other guard's feet as he aims at Boogeyman's exposed back. Using my knife, I stab his foot. He screams and kicks me in the face. I fall back to my ass, but within a second, I leap at him.

He tries to punch and slap me away. His mouth opens in a howl, but I attack like the feral animal they called me. I punch, pinning him down before lowering my head and biting his neck. I dig my teeth in, even as he fists my hair, trying to rip me away. The sharp tug of pain as he rips my hair out only encourages me, the skin in my teeth popping as I add more pressure, and then the sudden taste of blood fills my mouth.

Like the dog they made me, I jerk my head from side to side, widening the hole as he screams. I sit back, watching him cover the wound with a pale, astounded expression. Laughing, I slice my knife across his neck, watching the blood run from the lesion before rolling to avoid a man firing at me.

The guard snarls and swears as he picks me up by my hair. I scream random noises as I swipe out with my knife, hitting him in the gut. Over and over, I slice, driving him back until he releases my hair and his intestines spill from the giant wound I created.

Panting and covered in blood, I turn to see bodies scattered across the floor as Boogeyman finishes another off by stomping on his head. "See? We did good, part—" Something hard slams against the back of my head.

The last thing I see is the ground coming towards me as the darkness swallows me whole.

## CHAPTER EIGHTEEN

Idris

I'm not even winded, and my heart rate is slow and normal, but when I turn at her interrupted voice, adrenaline pumps through me. I watch her fall, her eyes closing as the man standing behind her grins at me. He holds a baton in his hand, which he used to club her over the head. She's lying motionless on the floor.

Dead or knocked out?

I'm not sure, but for some reason, rage fills me. The bored apathy I felt when I was killing these men disappears in an instant. My body heats, and my vision blurs with anger and the need to rip him apart. To kill him with my bare hands.

I don't remember moving.

I'm before him in an instant. He raises the baton towards me, but I catch it mid-air, watching as he strains, fighting against my grasp. I arch an eyebrow as he pants. His face turns red and sweat beads on his brow, but then I show him I was only playing with him. I snatch it from his hold and smash it across his face repeatedly.

He falls at some point, but I follow him down, caving in his skull and busting his eyeballs, smashing over and over until nothing but gore and shattered skull fragments remain. Chest heaving, I sit back and drop the baton to the floor with an audible bang. I'm just standing to check on her when I hear them coming up the stairs. Three sets of footsteps, in formation no doubt. I dive for the closest gun, and when they round the corner, I fire. I hit one before it clicks empty. Snarling, I get to my feet, ejecting the mag and grabbing another from a body and reloading before firing again. They manage to squeeze a shot off, but it goes wide, whereas mine do not.

All three are down.

I scan the room for any I may have missed and find one man groaning, trying to crawl to his gun. Rolling my eyes, I march over and slam my foot down on his arm. He screams and flips over, snot running from his nose. One of his eyes is sealed shut, and his lip is busted. Without warning, he spits, hitting my leg.

Kneeling over him, I shove my gun into his mouth, forcing it open as he groans and jerks beneath me. I narrow my eyes. "You shouldn't spit on people," I growl, and then I pull the trigger.

I leave the gun in the mess that was his head and walk over to the unconscious woman. I could kill her right now and tie up another loose end. Leave her body here so it looks like a breakout gone bad. Burn it all so no one finds her…

But I can't.

She fought, and she killed the guard who was trying to sneak up on me. I owe her my life. I hate that, but it's true. She's a warrior, she's more than a victim. She's a fighter, and she deserves her chance at revenge. Sighing, I lean down, grab her, and cradle her in my arms softly as I step over the bodies.

Leaving the room, I head downstairs, effortlessly carrying her. Down in the hallway, I find one more guard. He's hiding around a corner, and I stab him on the way past without waking her. I still have to get the other women, so I find the keys while I prop her against the wall in the corridor where they are located. Once I open the doors, they are terrified of me—screaming, crying, and begging. They are doing everything but fighting like my little bitch.

I nod, urging them to go, but when they don't, I snarl at them and they begin to run. They'll be fine. Picking her back up, I make sure they are all out before grabbing a hard drive I find. Another door draws my eye, and when I open it, I find myself in an auditorium of some sort with a pit below, the floor coated in blood. The seats are all empty, but it's clear something horrible happened here. This place needs to be destroyed.

Throwing her over my shoulder, I discover a small kitchen and turn the gas on before checking each and every room carefully for any survivors. I even pull the alarm to alert them, but no one else comes. The front door is unlocked, and as I'm heading through it, she begins to wake up. She's confused and begins to struggle on my shoulder, but I smack her ass to still her.

Once we're far enough away, I throw a lighter back inside. I place her on her feet on the cold, wet concrete in the parking lot as she blinks, keeping her hand in mine to steady her as we watch the building go up in flames.

"The women?" she asks, disoriented.

"Out."

She nods and looks at me. "How do we find them now?"

I flash her the drive, and she smiles before looking back at the burning structure. "You're free, you can go," I tell her.

She scoffs, keeping her gaze on the flames. "Not a chance, Boogeyman." She glances at me. "I want my revenge, like I said." She turns back to the fire as it roars. "I'm sticking with you for now."

A part of me likes that and wants her with me as I take these bastards down... I just don't know why. I don't trust easily, but for some strange reason, I trust this woman somewhat. Maybe because I see the same demons in her eyes that lurk in mine, or because her motives are the same. Either way, it has me breaking all my rules and doing something I've never done before.

"Idris," I growl over the sound of the flames and the distant sirens.

"Huh?" she asks, looking up at me. Her hand is still in mine, covered in blood, her once white shirt is now stained black and red, and her skin is coated in dirt and blood, her hair too. She's a beautiful wreck.

"My name is Idris," I tell her.

Her smile is slow, the fire reflecting in the deep depths of her gaze and crawling lovingly over her face. "Alena. Nice to meet you."

The building explodes.

# CHAPTER NINETEEN

### Alena

I*dris.* Strong. It fits him. I can't take my eyes off him as, with his hand still in mine, he hurries us from the explosion to a nearby parking lot. I should worry about the women, but honestly, I have more important things to deal with. Like hunting the bastards who did this to us. That's how I'll help them.

I watch, my mouth open, as he breaks the window of a car, opens the door for me, and then hot-wires it. We drive through the city as I sit sideways, watching him. "Where now?"

"First we need guns, and you need to clean and bandage those wounds," he rumbles as he switches lanes. I nod and go quiet for once, staring out of the window. I feel a bit faint, and my head is killing me. Ten minutes later, we pull up at what he tells me is Serenity, but to me it looks like a hospital. One of those old-style ones. Idris drives beneath the building, pulls into a parking garage, and presses his arm to the back of my seat as he reverses into the spot.

Fuck, why is that move so hot?

"Let's go," he mutters and gets out. I slide out after him, and he leaves the destroyed car in the middle of a bunch of sports cars and black Jeeps. It sticks out like a sore thumb, no doubt like I will, but Idris doesn't care. He drags me into an elevator, and within a moment, we rise. It stops at reception, and the door slides open. It's early morning, so not many people are here, but those who are turn and stare.

Not at him... at me.

Eyes widen, and people begin to whisper. I see pity and knowledge in their gazes, and it pisses me off. I snap my teeth at them. Idris reaches down and cuffs my neck, holding me as he leads me across the space to stop me from attacking anyone.

There's a perky blonde receptionist at a nice desk who starts to talk, but he ignores her and goes to another elevator, which opens as soon as we reach it. He pushes me in and stops before me with his arms crossed and eyebrows arched. I shrug and act like I don't care. Like everything isn't too bright, too loud. Escape was always my plan, but I never considered what it would be like out of that cell.

Or the way people would look at me and how it would make me feel.

Dirty, disgusting, ugly.

Like he can sense my thoughts, he moves closer, backing me into the wall. "Do not let them get to you. They don't know what it took for you to survive. Wear your badges of honour proudly," he murmurs softly, the kindest I've heard or seen him.

I nod, sucking down the self-loathing that sparked in me. Tilting my chin higher, I blow out a breath and let it wash over me. I'm not ashamed of what I've become to survive. Their opinions don't matter to me, and the fact Idris, the Boogeyman, is watching me with something akin to admiration and flaming desire pushes all those negative thoughts away.

The elevator stops moving and the doors open, but he doesn't step away until I crack a smile. "I'm fine," I murmur.

He lifts his hand and rubs his thumb along my cheekbone. "Want me to kill them for you?"

In that moment, I decide that even if it kills me, I'm going to fuck this man over and over again. The idea of him killing everyone for simply looking at me? Hot as hell. My pussy throbs as I imagine him doing just that as I stare into those serious eyes.

"Maybe later," I whisper, and his lips kick up at the side, even as we hear a throat being cleared. He keeps his eyes on me for a moment longer before turning and striding out of the elevator.

I follow after him and step into a living area. The ceilings are so high, I can barely see them, and there's a fancy as fuck open kitchen to my right. The living room is directly before us. Idris doesn't look around, he marches to the sofas where a man is sitting, watching us. He's an older man, a silver fox for sure. He's attractive, put together, and fancy. He has short, cropped grey hair with controlled stubble on his face. His bright, piercing blue eyes watch our every movement, and his muscular frame tugs at his fitted grey suit. He's built. I've never seen an older man with such muscle, but when I meet those cold eyes, I realise why. He's an assassin. It's in the calculating, cold way he watches us. Analysing, intelligent. I find my eyes darting around the penthouse just to avoid that unnerving gaze.

Who is this man? Why did Idris bring us here?

"There are women over at the docks, 843 Southwest," Idris begins as the man observes us.

"Hello to you too," he greets, sipping amber liquid from a crystal glass balanced on his knee. Encased in grey slacks and a button-up white shirt, he looks elegant, rich, and scary as shit. Beside him on the sofa, I see a picture, a flash of red before he covers it. "This one of them?" he asks and smiles at me. I think it's supposed to be reassuring, but I narrow my eyes.

"Name's Alena, not 'this,' asshole," I sneer. His eyebrows rise, a smile playing on his lips.

"My apologies," he offers, toasting the glass to me. "Alena."

Idris steps in front of me, crossing his arms and ignoring the question. "I need guns, and she needs medical assistance, then we'll be going."

I peer around him to see the man sigh. He sits forward as he drains his drink and places it on a gold coaster on the glass table before him. "And why do you need guns? I thought we discussed you staying retir—"

"I have no choice. They took me, so they will die," he snarls.

The man's eyebrows rise. "This complicates matters somewhat."

"How?" Idris demands.

"We are currently hunting them. This is our mission. It's why we told you to stay away from the city. You are crossing into another's assignment."

"Donald," Idris growls in warning. "They are dying, either you help or hinder me."

"If you do this—if you kill them, hunt them—are you ready for the consequences, Boogeyman?" Donald challenges as he stands, straightening his shirt as he steps closer. "Everyone will know you're back. You will be plunging right back into this world, and this time, there will be no escape, no retirement. You will leave only at the end of a gun. Think wisely. Is it worth sacrificing your hard-earned peace you so desperately craved?"

"I have no choice," Idris hedges, but he sounds resigned.

"Idris," I murmur, stepping around him. "You told me what it took to get free, don't do this. Let them kill them—"

I see Donald gaping at me in shock as Boogeyman turns, his expression thunderous as he steps closer, glaring down at me. Donald moves closer, almost panicked, as if to protect me. "Boogeyman, don't—"

I hold up my hand. "I can handle him," I mutter.

"You would give up your revenge?" he demands as he glares down at me. "You would give up the thought of what kept you alive?"

"Never." I sigh. "I'll kill them."

He snorts. "You'll take down an entire trafficking ring alone?"

"If I have to." I shrug. "Or I'll die trying."

"You chose your path, and so have I, little one. Do not question it again. I know my mind, I know the consequences," he murmurs, and then looks to Donald. "I have no choice, they die."

"So be it," he replies, but he seems almost sad. "You may kill them, hunt them if you wish... but not the American. Not the one at the top. He's mine."

"But—" Idris starts, and that's when I see the transformation in Donald. I thought he was scary before, but he is downright fucking terrifying now. His face goes cold, empty. Deadly. In those eyes, I see the truth. Idris can't hide what he is... but this man can. He conceals it well, but he's just as much of a killer as Boogeyman. I see the calculation in his gaze... the threat.

"Do not disobey my orders, Boogeyman. This is personal for you, but it is for me as well. Do not forget who put that gun in your hand, who watched your back, who gave you everything you wanted. Who offered you protection. This city is mine, and I say who dies and who lives. You may kill any other, but the American is off limits. If I find out you laid one finger on his head, you will be disavowed."

I don't know what that means, but it seems important, because Idris actually looks shocked. "You would remove me from the Clergy? You would make the hunter become the hunted? Order my death?"

"Yes," Donald replies without even blinking. "Do we have a deal?"

Reluctantly, Idris nods. "I still need supplies."

"And you will have them. Our services are open to you." He turns away before stilling. "Welcome back to the shadows, Boogeyman." He looks over his shoulder and meets my eyes. "Be careful who you walk in the darkness with, Alena." He purposely enunciates my name. "You may just find yourself in front of a gun instead of behind it."

With that, he pulls out a phone. "Send the doctor to my floor." He hangs up and dials another number while we watch. "Spider, come to chapel."

Donald returns his attention to Idris. "I assume you want that hard drive sticking out of your pocket checked over? He won't be long. Until then, you know where the priest is. You may leave Alena here for the doctor—"

"We stay together," I snap and turn to Idris. "Guns first, then doctor."

He looks down at me, his expression cold before a slow grin tugs at his lips as he shakes his head. "No, doctor first. You're useless to me if you get infected." He grabs the back of my neck again. "Behave, no biting or stabbing."

I roll my eyes but agree. Where is the fun in that?

# CHAPTER TWENTY

### Idris

The doctor won't take long to arrive, living in-house on the floor under Donald. He even has a surgery room there. And the ones who don't make it? Well, they go to the basement and the furnace room next to the mechanic shop and car stripping center.

Donald offers us a drink, and I force Alena to sip water and eat as much as she can. I do as well to keep my strength up. He watches us the entire time, which makes me narrow my eyes on him. He smirks. "Forgive me, I've just never seen you… care for another." I must make a noise because he chuckles and sits, taking a cup of tea. "Do not give me your murder face, Boogeyman. You know what I mean." His eyes flicker to Alena, and I look away, not listening.

"That's what I thought," he murmurs, but I hear it. "Alena, my dear, do you have any family looking for you?"

She stills, holding chicken in her bare, dirty hand halfway to her open mouth, which is filled with partially eaten food. It's even smeared across her face, but it just makes me grin at her savagery. Donald doesn't blink though, he's used to working with animals. She swallows before sitting back slightly and shakes her head.

"Friends?" he presses.

"By now, I'm betting they think I'm dead." She sighs. "I was taken a long time ago. My family died when I was young. I only have an uncle, but he wants nothing to do with me."

"How long?" he asks with a frown.

"I don't even know. I was sold originally, but it didn't work out." She grins. "I attempted to kill my buyer. They tried to resell me a lot after that, but it never worked out. They got tired of my… disobedience and just made me their men's plaything. Too long, would be my answer, but will the timeline change the trauma I endured? Will it make my torture less horrendous? So no, I don't know, and I don't want to know." She looks pointedly down at her body and back at him. "Even if they were looking, they should stop. The Alena who went to the club that night is dead."

"I see, I'm sorry," he offers and looks her over. "Do you wish to talk to someone about what happened?"

"Not unless it's a gun." She snorts and tears into the meat as he chuckles.

"It seems you have the same coping mechanism as many of my congregation. It's not a bad way to be, just make sure you don't lose yourself in the meantime," he remarks, unable to refrain from offering advice.

Just then, the elevator opens and the doctor appears. He goes to check me over, but I shake my head and jerk it at Alena. He freezes before looking at Donald, who waves him on. "Her fee will be covered by me, do not worry that she isn't a member." The old, hunched man who sewed me up more times than I can count but still never learned his name moves to her side. I watch him carefully as he examines her, tutting and muttering under his breath. He doesn't blanch at the scars or blood, and she slumps a little.

Was she worried?

He sews her up and plasters her toes and fingers. He pokes at her ribs before sighing as he stares at her stomach. "I can try to sew this—"

"No, just make sure it's not infected," she interjects at the same time I say, "No."

"Fine. What do I know? I'm just a doctor," he mutters but gets his kit out. She's given IV fluids, lots of tablets, and tests, including STD screenings, a pregnancy test, and normal bloodwork. She's actually quite healthy for someone who was held captive. She's malnourished of course, and underweight. Her bloodwork is a little insane, but she has no diseases, thank fuck. I didn't even consider that when I fucked her raw.

She allows him to do whatever he needs, but when he touches her stomach or near her pussy, she looks at me, as if I'm helping her focus on the present and not her memories. I make sure to stay close in case I need to kill him or stop him from triggering her.

After a few hours, he's done. He gives her tablets to take with her, ones that will keep her going while she hunts, the ones he gives injured assassins. He advises her against it, but she ignores him. I don't let him check me over, knowing I'm okay, and he leaves.

"Spider is almost here," Donald informs us. He's been working on his laptop the entire time. "He was dealing with a situation."

I wait in silence, knowing each moment that passes is another chance for them to escape. By now, they must have heard about the building blowing up. Will they stay or go? I'm betting they'll stay. If they have been fighting against Donald for this long, they have big balls and no plans to release their grasp on the city.

It doesn't stop me from pacing back and forth. I'm agitated and wanting to go, but we don't know where yet. Fucking Spider, what was so important he made us wait?

Just then, the elevator dings and the man in question steps out. There's blood on his suit, so that explains what he's been up to. He is excellent at getting information. I wonder if he was helping Donald or himself.

Either way, he's not someone I want to piss off.

"Spider, I need you to clean up Alena's past and trail please. Also, Boogeyman has a hard drive for you to look at," Donald tells him.

"So you're not dead." He winks at me as he strides over, the cocky fucker almost preening like a peacock in his three-piece suit with his perfect hair and model worthy face. I want to punch him so Alena won't look. "Though you did cause a mess with that explosion—

Alena?" he exclaims, gaping at her. He steps closer, looking her over intently, and I stand with a glare. "The Alena? It is, it's you."

She glances between us. "Do I know you?"

He shakes his head. "No, but my partner has been looking for you since you were taken."

"Why?" Alena queries, taken aback.

"She saw it happen." He sighs. "Thank fuck I can tell her you're okay. We thought you died. We found someone who bought you—"

She laughs. "Did he tell you he killed me? Please," she hisses. "I almost killed him. He was just annoyed a little girl overpowered him."

He laughs slightly, his eyes icy. "Either way, she will be relieved. When you have…" He glances over at me. "Finished whatever this is, you should meet her. I know she would be really happy."

She nods mutely, and he looks at me, taking the hint. "Hard drive?"

I hand it over, holding it firmly when he goes to grab it. "If you put her in danger, I'll kill you."

His eyebrow arches, and he glances at her—she's watching us intently—then back to me. "Understood." I let go, and he turns away, heading to set up and decode it and find out what he can.

Then, the hunt will begin.

# CHAPTER TWENTY-ONE

### Alena

While Spider is working, Idris takes me downstairs using the same elevator. I don't know what to think about some random woman looking for me, but Idris trusts these people, so I guess I should too, especially if they get me one step closer to those who took me in the first place.

One step closer to my revenge. It's all that's keeping me going. Moving.

My body feels better, strong almost. Whatever the doctor gave me in those pills and shots is doing the trick. My vision is clear, my hearing is better, and I have no pain at all. We don't stop at the same floor we came in on, no, the elevator opens into a chandelier lit hallway with wooden panels and deep maroon carpet. It screams expensive luxury. We pass a door that's partially open, and inside, I see what looks like body armour… and suits.

What the fuck is this place?

"Is this assassin headquarters?" I hiss.

Idris looks at me and smirks. "Headquarters? I guess. We have hundreds of locations around the world. It's a safe zone for people like us to restock and rest. We can also connect with a member of the Clergy who is part of the leadership, like Donald."

"Shit, this is badass," I reply as we stop at a gold double door at the end. He swings it open, and I shit you not, a man with slicked back hair, garbed in a three-piece penguin suit, with a beard down to his shoulders, turns. He's tall and skinny, but there is something about him that sets me on edge.

It could be the rows upon rows of weapons in this fucking room. There are LED lit tables with guns, swords, knives, and a fucking rocket launcher perched on them. Along each wall is every weapon you could ever imagine, from grenades to fucking garrottes.

"Mr. Boogeyman, how lovely to see you again," he greets. "May I be of assistance?" His voice is deep but smooth.

"Hello, Priest," Idris responds, before leaning towards me and whispering, "Don't look too closely at him. He's one of the best assassins of our time. He retired, and Donald made him head of arms here. He used to be the right-hand man of the Clergy. He knows more secrets than you could imagine, not to mention he could kill us before we blink." He straightens, and addresses Priest once more. "I need weapons, lots of weapons."

"Very good, sir. Will you be starting with party favours or the main course?" he replies instantly, moving his hands behind his back.

"All. Pack up some specials for dessert too. Semis, rifles, and handguns mainly. Big calibre with stopping power and plenty of extra mags. I'll choose some of my own as well." Idris nods.

"Very good. I will get right on that. If you need help, don't hesitate to alert me." He nods and turns, grabs two large black duffel bags, and methodically begins loading them with God knows what.

"Pick your weapons," Idris tells me. "I will put you under my membership," he declares and walks away, leaving me gawking and wondering where to start.

Biting my lip, I feign confidence and head to the first wall of guns I see. There are big automatic weapons and rifles, but at the bottom are handguns, and I run my fingers across them until I stop at a small black one at the end.

I jump when I feel hands on my hips, large hands as a hard, hot body presses against my back. I shiver from his proximity, my whore pussy demanding his attention, but we have more important things to do.

"Do you like that one? It's a Beretta, a good gun," he whispers, moving his hands from my hips and up my arms to where I'm rotating the gun. "Steady without too much recoil. It's a good choice and fits your hand."

I nod, and he leans closer, running his nose along my skin. "Good girl." He moves away, and I take a desperate breath. "We will take as many knives and close contact weapons as you can pack, as well as all the small calibre handguns there. Give me a few remote explosives too, and a rifle, you know my preferences."

"Very good. I will have it waiting for you at reception. Will you be needing transport? I can contact the garage for you."

"Yes, give me shielded storm power," Idris replies as he grabs me and pulls me to his side.

"Of course, it will be done." Idris turns and pulls me to the door, but the man's voice stops us. "It is a pleasure, as always, sir. May I say it's a joy to see you back?"

"Thank you," Idris responds and pulls me back out into the corridor.

If Idris fears Priest, and he respects Idris and his skills, just how much of a fucking terror is the man holding my hand?

---

HE MAKES ME STOP AT THE TAILOR AS WELL. A CURVY, BEAUTIFUL woman who's dressed like a fifties pin-up girl runs it. She makes me feel strong and sure and doesn't blink over my scars as she finds what I need. I end up with a vest as well as braces, a couple of holsters, some badass steel toed boots, and hair ties which can be used as garrottes. Over it all are some black trousers, a black tank, and a leather jacket that matches Idris's.

She allows me to shower in the back of the shop, and after, she pins my hair up, explaining how they can be used as weapons too. All the while, Idris dresses, smirking at me when he sees me giving him a glare. He chooses black cargo trousers, a skintight black shirt, a leather jacket with matching boots, and more carriers and holsters than I can count. She doesn't even try to help him, instead almost avoiding him, and when she looks at him, there is a glint of fear in her eyes, but she never lets it show. She's efficient and courteous, and when she shows me how to reload a gun and throw a knife, my impression of her rises.

It seems everyone here is trained and skilled… apart from me. But that isn't stopping me or even Idris.

Once we're done, we go back to the penthouse where Spider and Donald are waiting for us. Spider stands behind Donald, who is seated with another cup of tea. Does this man do nothing but drink? "We have what you need," Spider says instantly. "It won't be easy, but then again, you like a challenge." He smirks.

"Remember the deal, the American is ours, you can have the rest," Donald reminds us.

Idris nods as I stand there.

"I have addresses, cars, and current locations for you. If they change, I will text you," Spider offers and then looks at me. "Don't die, my girl would kick my ass."

Unsure what else to say, I just agree, and we leave with the list, riding down the elevator in silence. When we reach the garage, a black SUV is waiting for us, and when I peek in the back seat, I see the bags of weapons as well as food and water and spare clothing.

It's everything we need to hunt people across the city.

## CHAPTER TWENTY-TWO

### Idris

It seems some of them got spooked and ran. Others? Not so much. In fact, they are spread out in public as if to make a point, or they simply don't care. That will be their downfall.

You can't hide or run from Boogeyman.

"Which one first?" I offer her the list. It has some mug shots and social media pictures with information. She flips through the pictures and stops on a blond man, her eyes narrowed and nostrils flared. She looks at me with an expression even I wouldn't want to be on the other end of.

"Him."

I face forward and start the engine, following the details on the form. It lists his home location, a two-story house in a bad neighbourhood. It takes us around an hour to get through the morning traffic to get there. Graffiti coats the walls, rubbish is scattered on the ground, houses are boarded up, and there's even a burnt car on the corner. I park on the next street over from the house and look at her.

"Ready?"

She doesn't answer but gets out. I follow and watch as she pulls a giant knife from her hip, twisting it as she storms towards the address.

Eyes alert, I follow her. She doesn't even knock on the door, she just tries the handle and then snarls when it's locked. I move her to the side and kick the door in.

It flies open with a bang, wood splintering everywhere. There's a crash upstairs as she rushes in, her eyes wild as she turns her head before spotting the half broken wooden staircase to the left. She takes the steps two at a time. Sighing, I place the door back in place so passers-by don't call the police and follow after her at a slower pace, my boots loud.

I hear a scream before it's cut off. I follow it down the hallway, passing two open doorways. One to a bathroom, the other to an empty room. The last door is to a bedroom. There are beer bottles, empty vodka bottles, and used needles scattered all over with clothes thrown here, there, and everywhere. But there is a giant flat screen TV, probably stolen, in the corner of the room.

In the wooden double bed lies the blond man. He's already bleeding with Alena perched on his chest, her knife digging into his bare skin. He's staring up at her in shock, but it turns into a snarl as he tries to throw her. I'm there in an instant, my gun pointed at his head. "Don't move," I order.

He freezes, his eyes going to me, and in his gaze, I see the knowledge he will die here, he knows what I'm capable of, and that if I come for you, you die. But it's not me he should be worried about, because I know this is the man who carved his name into her stomach, and from the way she's watching him, it makes me think she wants to return the favour.

Keeping my gun aimed at his head, I grab a wooden chair pushed against the wall, turn it, and straddle it. "Continue," I tell her.

She looks over at me with a bloodthirsty grin, the sight going straight to my cock. Groaning, I rearrange my hard-on and watch as she rips away the sheet covering him, leaving him naked. He tries to slap her, but I fire my gun in warning, hitting the pillow next to him, which explodes in feathers, and he freezes. "Next time, it goes through your kneecap."

"I just wanted to say hi," Alena taunts and presses her hand to the top of the knife handle, pushing the blade deeper until he gasps and blood drips across his pale, skinny chest. Droplets stain his skin ruby red before rolling down his side and dropping to his white bedding. She releases the pressure and leans closer. "I figured we could finish playing. You got to have your fun, but I didn't get to have mine."

He tries to speak, exposing his mutilated tongue, so instead, he glares at her and mouths, "Crazy." She backhands him, the slap so loud it rings out and his head is whipped to the side.

"I'm not crazy!" she screams and then flips her hair over her shoulder. Alena slowly moves the knife down his chest to his stomach, right above his quivering belly. "Don't be rude."

I watch as she drags the knife down, a hiss leaving her lips when it splits the skin and blood wells. With a crazed look, she slides it back up, deeper, slicing him open. He screams and struggles, but she keeps going. Alena laughs as blood coats her knife, her hands, her arms, and her face. She slices and slices intently, his screams growing increasingly louder as she pins him down.

I watch the way the bright red coats her skin, the way her lips part on a moan, and my desire grows. His screams only egg me on as I lean farther forward, grinding my erection into the chair. She shifts back then, and I grin when I spot what she carved.

DOG.

He lies there panting, his eyes rolling around desperately as sweat drips down his pale face. "Who's the dog now?" She spits on him, then grins wider. With a quick wink at me, she stabs the knife down, right through the O, and she twists and grinds it as he passes out. It's a killing blow, bleeding heavily, ensuring he will die slowly and painfully. Pulling back, she tosses the knife to the bed and slides from his body to the floor.

I push up from the chair and kick it away, frowning when she drops to her hands and starts to crawl, leaving bloody handprints on the wood as she moves.

She stops, gets to her knees before me, and meets my eyes. With bloody hands, Alena reaches out to tug at my trousers. "What?" My question ends in a groan when she deftly frees my cock and grips my hard length. Her tongue darts out and licks along those pink, bloody lips as she blinks innocently up at me, but she can't hide the insanity, bloodlust, and desire in those depths.

"I want you," is all she says before leaning down and swallowing me whole. Her hand strokes down at the same time to squeeze my base, and I widen my stance, reaching down to anchor my hand in her black hair. I'm unable to deny her when I've been hard as a rock this entire time and imagining the same thing. She squeezes harder, so hard it hurts, and fuck if I don't almost explode. My eyes shut and my head falls back as I allow myself a moment of vulnerability and slam into that hot, naughty mouth, forcing my huge length down her throat. She chokes, and when I look down, tears roll from her eyes and down her cheeks.

The sight is too much.

Pulling free, I reach down, grab her, and toss her onto the bloody, messy bed right next to her dying torturer. He's awake now, gasping for breath as he bleeds out. Knowing he's watching? That he's dying? It has me harder than ever, my cock dripping with her saliva and my precum. She bounces when she hits the mattress before pushing up and flinging herself at me. Snarling, I catch her mid-air and throw her back again, and this time, I pin her until she stills before flipping her and dragging her ass into the air.

Grabbing the knife from the bed, I quickly slice through the crotch of her trousers and panties, exposing her glistening pink pussy. Her greedy hole clenches as she pushes back, struggling in my hold to get what she wants.

Dragging the bloody knife across her ass, I dip it down to her pussy, and she freezes. "Keep fighting, and I'll fuck you with it, understood? Blood and all."

She moans, pressing back to try and take the knife, and my eyes nearly cross. Holy fuck. I tighten my hold on her hips, keeping her still so I don't rip her in half before slowly pressing the tip of the bloody knife to her dripping cunt—close enough so she can feel the threat, but far enough away so it won't hurt her. She shivers in my hold, crying out.

"More!" she demands. I don't move it, and she snarls, fighting in my grip again, almost cutting herself as I grunt, my cock throbbing at the picture before me—the knife almost inside her tight pussy as blood mixes with her cream and drips down her cunt to her engorged clit.

With a snarl, she pushes back, trying to impale herself on the knife, but I rip it away and toss it aside before grabbing a small one at my hip, pressing the wide leather handle to her pussy. She wants to fuck it? She can. I hold it still for her as she moans. She doesn't seem to care, panting and groaning with her face pressed against the bed as she pushes back, taking the handle as far as she can and fucking herself on it. Reaching down, I flick her clit over and over again as she moans, grinding softly, and with a scream, she comes all over the leather. I pull it free as she does, and her cum drips from her pussy hole as I watch.

She falls forward as I release her, turning her head to look at me as I bring the knife up. Keeping my eyes on her, I flatten my tongue and drag it down the handle, tasting her and the blood as she heaves for air. I drop it, bend down, and run my tongue along her pink pussy and dip it inside her until she's grinding against my face.

Dragging it back up her pussy, I keep going straight to her asshole, circling it over and over again as she cries out, and then I stand up and stroke my cock, watching her—ass up, pussy dripping and bloody, her body spread before me like a fucking feast as the man takes his last breath. A death rattle. I grab her and slam into her cunt.

She screams and claws at the bedding but thrusts back to take my cock deeper. I watch her hole stretch around my girth, her blood and cum coating it as I pull out and hammer back in, pushing her forward on the bed from the force.

I hear sirens in the distance. Even if they shoot me or try to arrest me, I'm not leaving her cunt until I'm good and done. Let them come. I smash into her, her screams getting loud as she clenches around me, gripping my cock so tightly I have to force myself through her channel.

I lift her from the bed and slam her into the wall. She snarls, and I pull from her pussy. The wet sound is loud as I spin her and smash her into it again. Her head hits the wall, and she stutters out a breath, even as she grabs my shoulders and yanks me closer, wrapping her legs around me as she tries to impale herself on my cock again.

I line up and thrust in, making her scream, our breaths mixing. Her eyes are closed, her mouth open as she pants. Her chest and face are flushed as she pushes back against the wall for leverage and starts riding my cock.

The sirens get louder, but it only adds to the pleasure. She doesn't care either, slamming herself down on me unashamedly, her cream coating my balls. But when she leans forward and bites my lip, dragging it out…

I lose all logic.

I throw her across the room, and she sails through the air, hitting the TV and shattering it. Storming over, I grab her, bend her over, and plunge back inside of her. I force her into an awkward angle as I grab her pussy from behind, holding it tight as I hammer into her. The pleasure is too much, racing up and down my spine. With a roar, I come, exploding inside her, and she screams her own release as we hear the cars skid to a stop outside the house.

Pulling free, I watch my cum drip from her for a second before throwing her over my shoulder.

I grab the knife and quickly check over the scene before heading to the window which overlooks the back garden. It's overgrown and filled with rubbish and surrounded by a rusted chain fence with holes in it. Opening the window, I throw one leg out and then balance on the edge as I hear them come in the front door. I jump and land on my feet, bending to absorb the impact, and then I'm up and sprinting in a second, leaping over the fence and into the abyss of the destroyed neighbourhood.

They will never find us.

Only his body.

The first name on our list.

# CHAPTER TWENTY-THREE

## Alena

The spare clothes come in handy. When we get back to the car, I rip off my ruined trousers and wipe the cum and blood away as best as I can. Idris drives off into the night as I stretch into the back, my stomach twinging as I grab more clothes and slip into them commando. He hands my knife over as he manoeuvres the vehicle. I wipe it clean and sigh, a smile on my face as he cranks up the heat.

"Who's next?" I ask.

He smiles and turns the wheel, drifting around a corner. "I've already picked. Spider texted me, he's close."

I shrug and watch the roads as we speed from the scene. He weaves through the evening traffic, and before long, we pull up into a multi-storey parking garage. He takes us nearly all the way to the top to a darkened, closed in floor. The lights flicker overhead, providing hardly any illumination, and the sunlight doesn't reach this far. This level is mostly empty, filled with a few expensive Mercs.

He stops in the corner and gets out.

I follow, and he heads over to a silver Audi in the corner, checking the reg before pulling a key from his pocket and pushing it. It doesn't look like a normal key though, and he sees my expression. "I have my tricks." He smirks and opens the back door. "In." He gestures.

I crawl in, and he spanks me on the way before following after. He sits low in the back seat, a gun ready in his hand as he shuts the door and gets comfy. His eyes close as he leans his head back against the headrest.

"What now?" I question.

"Now?" he murmurs, turning his head and opening one eye. "We wait. Sleep while you can."

He relaxes back, and the car is silent. I look around, but I decide *fuck it*. He's right, I'm tired, and I may as well nap while we wait. Curling into the seat, I press my cheek to the expensive leather seat and close my eyes.

I'm asleep before I can even count to five.

---

I WAKE WARM AND COMFY. I CRACK OPEN AN EYE TO FIND MY HEAD pressed against his chest. His arm is around me, and my hands are clutching his shirt.

He's unmoving and silent, his chest rising and falling slowly. He's asleep. I take the moment to run my gaze over his face. The old, faded scars make me ache to reach out and touch them. I wouldn't dare while he was awake, since he would probably throw me from the car or shoot me, but something about the peace, the silence on his face, has me reaching up. Darting my eyes between his closed ones and his cheek, I slowly reach towards it. Before my fingers can even make contact, he grabs my wrist tightly, grinding the bones until I gasp.

His eyes open, and his breathing never changes as his head slowly turns. Idris's dark eyes lock on me as his lips tilt down. "What are you doing?" he rumbles in warning, his deep, gravelly tone sending a shockwave of lust straight to my pussy.

"I just wanted to touch you," I murmur. He watches me, unblinking, squeezing tighter and tighter until I think he might break my wrist, but then he suddenly lets go. The shock of it makes my hand drop. Not once does he look away, but his eyes are guarded and his body is tense, like he's expecting me to try and kill him or hurt him as I inch closer.

Poor man.

If all you know is pain, you begin to expect it from everyone. It becomes easier to be guarded, to never be vulnerable. I see it in his eyes—the lack of trust.

The anticipation for the blow.

Humans are such fragile creatures. Our bodies can withstand damage, but it's our hearts, our minds that bear the scars, even after the bones have set and the skin has healed. And Boogeyman? His mind is filled with scars, a thousand tiny cuts. All reminders of what humans are capable of.

For some reason, I want to change that, I want to heal one of those wounds to prove we aren't all bad. To offer even a semblance of peace to this man who helped bring me back from the brink and gave me everything I needed.

Wanted.

I may be damaged. I may be crazy and fucked up. I may never have a normal life again, or find love and happiness, but that doesn't mean all of the old me is gone. There are hints of her, of the woman who used to volunteer at the dog shelter every weekend, who brought food to the homeless shelter, who would smile and pay for someone's bill if they were struggling. The darkness they injected into me with each blow, each act of violation and degradation, can only infect so much.

Even the night has glimmers of light, like the stars lighting up the dark.

I move my hand slowly so I don't spook him, acting as I would with the abused, untrusting dogs they brought in. I always went to the ones who were labelled as biters and broken beyond repair. No animal or human is. You simply have to be patient, kind, and willing to get bit, but when they trust you, when they open up and show you what's beneath all that anger…

Hate.

Pain.

There is such love, such kindness and devotion, it makes it all worthwhile. I wonder if he's the same, or is my assassin dark to the core? I don't think he is, although he's no saint. His hands are covered in so much blood that I bet he can almost see it, his soul stained from the crimes he's committed. Yet I see glimpses of something more. Like when he took the pain away from me, or when he let me kill my torturer or saved me from Donald and the doctor. Like now, as he waits silently, unmoving, to give me what I want, even though it might hurt him.

I touch his skin, and he jerks slightly before holding still. I scan his face to make sure he's okay before running the very tips of my fingers across his cheek, feeling the raised edges of his scars. "They feel like mine," I whisper as I lower my touch to the edge of his jaw line, noticing one runs completely across it. "What happened?"

"I was captured deep in the jungle and held in a war camp. They tried to skin me," he murmurs, holding still as I trace my nail across it and then up his chin to his lips. They part slightly, and his warm breath brushes against my skin as I run my fingers across the plump softness. My gaze rises to his to see he's watching me, his eyes darkening with desire.

I freeze, both of us unmoving, just caught in each other's gazes.

We burst into movement. My hands clasp his face, and our lips smash together as he groans. I swallow it down before getting to my knees on the expensive leather seats, gripping his cheeks as I kiss him. He grabs my hips and drags me onto his lap so I'm straddling him. My hips roll, rubbing across his hardening cock as I whimper into his talented mouth. His hand reaches for my trousers, yanking them open as his fingers dive inside of them. He cups my wet pussy as I rub against him, back and forth until he pulls away from my mouth.

"You have ten seconds to get naked and on my dick," he growls out.

My eyes widen, and he smirks.

"Ten."

Fuck. I leap from his lap, desperately yanking at my pants as he leans back and opens his jeans as he watches me. "Nine."

I get my trousers down, but I almost fall trying to get them over my boots. "Eight," he murmurs as he strokes his cock. "Seven."

I finally get them off and straddle him again. "Six, five, four, three, two, one," I offer as I grab his cock and slam down on it.

He groans as I hiss, working him into me. I only get a few inches before I have to lift and drop again. I grab the headrest, digging my nails in to gain leverage as I grind and lift. His eyebrow arches. "Are you on my cock, Alena?" he challenges dangerously. I whimper, even as I shake my head.

"I'm trying," I reply as I drop farther down, getting him halfway in. "I'm not wet enough, and you're too big," I defend.

He narrows his eyes, letting me know he's not pleased with my answer as his hand comes up. I watch with rapt fascination, speared on his cock, as he spits into his palm and then reaches down. I rise, and he covers his cock in his saliva before shoving his fingers inside of me alongside his cock, making me groan in both pain and ecstasy as my eyes close.

He stretches me before pulling his fingers free, and then he grabs my hips and slams me down, making me cry out as he bottoms out. The flash of pain fades when he starts to move, thrusting up and grunting as he does. Our breaths mix as the car starts to steam up, rocking with the force of our movements as he fucks me hard and fast.

I'm oblivious to everything other than him—the feeling of his thick shaft piercing me, his huge hands gripping me harshly, his scent invading my nostrils.

He suddenly pulls me off, spins me, and slams me back down on his cock. My eyes fly open, looking through the partition of the seats and the front window, but he just carries on fucking me leisurely, hard, and fast, like he has all the time in the world.

I relax back, rolling my hips to meet his thrusts, wetter than ever now as pleasure flows through me. Like a circuit, back and forth, making me wild.

Needy.

"Don't stop," he orders, even as he grabs his gun and points it over my shoulder. A moment later, the front door unlocks and a man in a suit gets in. The door slams shut as I shiver, still riding Idris's cock as he slides the safety off and moves the gun over the seat and against his head.

"Don't fucking move," Idris snarls as he slaps my hip, urging me on. "Hands on the wheel. We'll be with you in a minute."

He keeps the gun against the man's head as I ride his cock, twisting and groaning. I lean my head back as he flicks my nipples through my shirt before gripping my neck.

I watch as the man's eyes flicker up to the rearview mirror, his hands still on the wheel. His scared, panicked breathing is loud, even over the wet squelch of our bodies moving together and my moans. I meet his blue orbs and smirk as I grind down hard, impaling myself on Idris's giant cock. His eyes widen and roam down my body before he quickly looks away.

"Do not fucking look at her," Idris snaps behind me, leaning forward to slap the gun across the man's head before sitting back. The change in angle has me groaning and my pussy clenching as I reach for that peak I feel coming. His hold tightens on my neck in warning for encouraging the man.

It's what sends me over the edge. I gasp my release as his hand flexes on my vulnerable throat, his fingers digging into the sides until I see black. He slams up into me over and over until he grunts, stills, and fills me with his release as I shiver with aftershocks. The pleasure batters me like the waves of the ocean. Slumping back, I run my fingers down to my pussy and just sit there, watching the man.

"Who are you?" the man asks, eventually breaking the silence. He's not familiar to me, but Idris seems to know who he is.

"You're the banker for the trafficking operation, correct?" Idris rumbles, unbothered that I'm draped across him as he interviews this guy.

He stays silent, and Idris prods him with the gun.

"Don't make me prove how serious I am. You are the banker, correct?"

"Yes," he replies hesitantly. "But they will kill me if—"

"Why does everyone say that? Motherfucker, I'll kill you and your family too. If you want your two daughters and wife to survive, I suggest you tell me where the money is held."

He glances back at us before pressing his head against the wheel, shaking. "I can't," he sobs.

"123 Winchester Boulevard," Idris snaps. "That's your home, isn't it? What a lovely family you have—"

"Okay, okay!" he yells. "Just don't hurt them, please, they're innocent. They think I just work here at the bank, but I couldn't turn down the money on the side."

"Nor the drugs and free stolen girls," Idris snarls. "Location."

The man reels it off, and Idris, without a second thought, pulls the trigger. The shot is loud, making me jerk. I watch as his head explodes, his blood and brain matter splattering across the wheel and front window, which shatters slightly.

"Get dressed, time to go," he murmurs to me.

I swallow and nod, pulling myself from his cock with a wince before climbing out of the car. I slip into my trousers as he shuts the door and checks over the car before doing something to the petrol cap. Taking my hand, he leads me back to the SUV and helps me in. He starts the engine, and just as we are pulling away, I hear the Audi explode.

Another one down.

## CHAPTER TWENTY-FOUR

Idris

We find the church they are using to hold the money, and we burn the stack, cutting them off at the source. It will piss them off and act as another warning. We are hunting them, nothing is safe from us.

We waste no time. We want to hit as many as we can before they spook and run. It will be harder to track them down then, whereas if they are all still in the city, it makes it easier. The news should filter through to some, but not all, before we get there, so I choose the farthest away for our next target. Not a lowly guard, but an investor. One who buys lots of girls and lets the traffickers use his clubs to help kidnap them.

Spider had a lot of people and details. It seems they were seriously investigating this before we came along. But now I'm the clean-up, and I'm good with that. They can focus on the American, the leader, while we take out everyone else who they haven't already killed. This list is missing a lot of key players, so they must be dead.

This next one requires a change of clothing, or we won't be admitted otherwise. Being an assassin is all about being adaptable. I may be huge and scary looking, which isn't always the best for covert missions, but I have to be able to blend in when needed.

Like now.

Alena has to as well. She protests but then relents when I tell her it's the only way to get to him. We hit the nearest shop, and money isn't an object. I leave her to find suitable attire and select a suit. Luckily they have my size because I've used them before, and any shop the Clergy does business with knows to stock well. When I get back, buttoning the last part of my jacket, I still, my mouth drops open, and my heart skips.

She's indescribable.

I've never seen her in a dress. She still looks better naked and covered in blood, but holy fuck. I may have to kill anyone who looks at her. She's in a tight, form-fitting red dress. It's deep red, like the colour of fresh blood, and the material is silk, draping enticingly across her curves. There's a split up both sides, unashamedly showing off her skin and scars. The dresser is well mannered enough not to comment or look at them as Alena turns, checking out the back in a mirror. It's backless, exposing her skin before the fabric begins just above her ass. Fuck, she looks good enough to eat. Her hair is combed and wavy instead of a mess, falling over one shoulder.

A gold flower holds the side back.

She must hear me because she looks over her shoulder, meeting my eyes. "I used to dress like this before. Now I feel like a Barbie doll," she says with a scoff.

"But a fuckable Barbie." I smirk as I run my gaze down her form. "Though I prefer chains and blood."

The saleswoman doesn't even blink, wearing a fake smile on her face. I dismiss her with a nod. "Thank you, please charge it to my card and take a generous tip."

"Of course, sir," she replies and rushes away, letting me know she's uncomfortable. Alena turns, steps down from the podium, and strides over to me, comfortable in the heels and dress. It's obvious she's worn them before, even though she already told me. Each step reveals the length of her toned thighs all the way to her hips. She stops before me, smirking as she raises her chin. She reaches out and runs a nail down my suit-clad chest.

"You clean up nice too, though I prefer the bloodstained, holey jeans and your bare chest," she purrs, her eyes alight with desire as her hand slips lower and cups my cock. I arch my eyebrow, checking the clock, but we don't have time.

"Later," I promise, grabbing her hand and tucking it through my arm. "We have a show to attend. I heard the ending will be killer," I joke.

She grins. "Then by all means," she replies.

---

THE SHOW IS ALREADY UNDERWAY WHEN WE ARRIVE, THE INTERVAL just finishing. I spot our mark instantly, sitting near the back in the wings with empty seats around him. In fact, the whole row is empty. It wouldn't surprise me if he booked them all. His daughter is performing, after all.

Alena squeezes my hand and lets go, sauntering behind the row to the other end as I walk towards him. He doesn't notice us, concentrating on the stage where they are dancing. The lights are low and the music is loud. He turns as I sit next to him, an annoyed expression on his thin face.

"That seat is booked," he snaps as Alena sits on his other side, holding a blade in her hand. She digs it into his ribs, making him jerk and frantically look around before focusing back on me.

"Not anymore," she retorts.

I turn to partially face the stage as his eyes narrow. He stops panicking, swallowing it back, and shows us exactly what kind of man he is as he relaxes in his chair, his voice low and pissed. There isn't even a tremor of fear, he's more annoyed at the interruption. I'm betting he's regretting giving his guards a day off. "What do you want?"

"You know what we want," she snarls, and with her eyes on me, she leans closer, pressing her breasts to his arm and licking the shell of his ear. "Your pain, your death."

"Who are you?" he demands.

"Ghosts," I reply, even as Alena says, "Your worst enemies."

I glare at her, and she licks a long line down his face. He flinches, even as I reach over and push her back into her chair. "Touch him again, and I'll be causing a scene. Understood, Bitch?"

She pouts but sits back, twisting the knife in her hands and making her fingers bleed. The man glances over and gags before quickly looking away while she giggles.

"What the fuck is wrong with her?" he asks. His eyes are on the stage, but his full focus is on her, like he dare not look too long in case she pounces on him.

"There's nothing wrong with her, she's perfect," I snarl, swapping my gun for a knife and pressing it against his side.

She sighs. "You think I'm perfect?" she murmurs romantically.

I roll my eyes then glare at her, but she smiles warmly as I focus back on him. "We know who you are and what you've done. We want nothing from you but your death. It will be a message to them."

"What message?" he queries, even as he pales, knowing he has no way out. He tries to stand, but I push him down.

"That we are coming for them," I answer as the music reaches a crescendo. The room is almost pitch black except for the exit signs. Every eye is on the stage except for ours as people gasp at the show.

Him? He cries out in pain as I stab him with the knife, making sure to hit many organs, including his lung. It fills with blood. He will choke on it, giving him a slow, painful death. I narrow my eyes on him.

"Enjoy the show," I tell him as I stand, pocketing the knife. I proffer my hand to Alena. She takes it and straddles the man's lap, leaning down and kissing his bloody, bubbling lips as he falls to the side.

"She truly is talented," she comments, and then we leave him there with his eyes fixed on the stage where his daughter dances with such emotion. A goodbye to her lover in the story, a goodbye to her father in real life as he lies dying in the stands.

His last image is of the only woman he never abused.

Delivered by one he did and the man he ordered dead.

We leave the theatre hand in hand. As soon as I get to the car, I strip, changing back to my tactical gear while Alena watches. She's draped across the back seat, her legs spread as she flips through the remaining papers. Her eyes come to me every now and again.

"Who now?"

"Bessie," is my response.

She grins and sits up, the papers drifting to the seat as she leans forward and hooks her fingers in my belt to drag me closer. The only reason I move is because I want to. I press my hands to the hood of the car as I lean down. Her mouth opens and she shifts closer, kissing the section of exposed skin between my jeans and shirt.

A shiver goes through me, and pleasure shoots down my spine until I ache to grab that teasing mouth and force it onto my cock. But Bessie is now a target, meaning she's out in public, vulnerable. We move now or we lose her to the wind.

"Can I watch while you torture her?" she requests silkily.

I have to close my eyes before I give in to temptation. Her. "Yes," I snarl.

"She's the one you want most, right?" she asks as she slips from the car, pushing me back as her body slides along mine. She still has to tilt her head back to see me though. "She betrayed you, used you. Don't go easy on her just because you think you should. She may be a woman, but she's a fucking cunt."

"Bitch," I snap, grabbing her chin. "I don't go easy on anyone. I don't give a fuck if they have a pussy or two goddamn mythical cocks. She will pay with her screams and blood."

Her eyes flare as she leans farther into my touch. "Good." Her tongue licks over her ruby lips. "I can't wait to see it. Show me the creature they all fear, show me the man even assassins have nightmares of, and after, fuck me in the carnage."

*Fuck.*

# CHAPTER TWENTY-FIVE

### Alena

I change out of the dress the old me would have loved. The expensive material, the confidence it brought. I would have gotten free drinks all night and taken some rando home. Now? All I can think about is how easily it can be stained and how hard it is to move in if I need to run or grab a weapon.

I did look fucking good though, scars and all, and Idris's reaction made it all worthwhile. But now I'm back to being Bitch, the words carved into my stomach acting as proof. I pop more of the doctor's pills and down some water. We aren't stopping or resting until this is done. The adrenaline of getting payback against all those who hurt me and thousands of others spurs me on.

Some of the names we get are crossed off—dead. Spider's and Max's work, whoever he is, apparently. We are the clean-up, catching the stragglers and the hard to find ones. And, of course, Nikolić, who we're saving for last.

Idris grabs his phone, dials someone, and simply grunts before hanging up. "She's still there, cameras confirm it. She's booked the entire restaurant. She was meeting with someone, but they've left," he informs me, and the look he gives me is downright terrifying and sexy as hell. With a twist of the wheel, he slams on the gas, racing through the evening traffic.

Hard to think that just last night I was still a captive, a stolen girl, and now I'm the hunter.

The feeling is heady, and when we pull up outside the restaurant, I can't help the grin I'm wearing or the excitement coursing through my veins. I feel invincible with Idris, untouchable. A girl could get used to this.

There's a valet in a suit outside, and he frowns when we pull in. "I'm afraid we are closed, sir," he starts, but Idris just storms past him without a glance.

"Sir," he snaps, and reaches for his phone. Me? I walk past and bitch-slap him.

"Oops, sorry." I grin innocently before turning and finding Idris watching me from the doors. His eyes move from the man to me as he grins and draws his gun.

"Be ready for anything, try not to get shot," is all he says as he turns and rips open the door. I follow after him, Beretta in hand. He begins shooting as soon as he enters, walking through the restaurant like a man would walk through fire. A haze of bullets rains down, as well as shouts and commands from Bessie the cow's security.

She's obviously special to Nikolić and the operation. Probably gets the women in, the cunt. It seems apt she will die by the man she thought she tricked. The bitch was too cocky.

I stay behind Idris, using him as a shield. The restaurant is one of those fancy ones with glass windows all around and simple, rustic tables with chandeliers. It's almost blacked out with low lighting and luxurious gold and black décor. It screams money and elitism. To the right is a glass staircase, and I see two men in suits sneaking down it, so I center myself, aim, and fire. I hit the glass under one, and it shatters, making him fall.

Shit.

"Good shot," Idris calls, and I just nod like I meant to do that all along. I fire at the other, missing three times before I hit him in the chest and he tumbles down the stairs. Turning back, I duck the swing of another man, and then Idris is there, pistol-whipping him before he flips him over his shoulder and onto a table, and in the same move, Idris stabs down with his gun and shoots before whirling to face the others streaming into the room.

We hear the waiters' screams as they rush out of the back door into the kitchen. I'm betting Bessie cow is hiding upstairs, stupid woman. Clearly, she can only be tough when her enemies are chained. Idris moves across the room fluidly, firing and taking as many out as he can before dropping his clip and reloading in mere seconds. He swings a shotgun around and fires, each move calculated, purposeful, hitting its intended target.

He moves like fucking water.

I turn and slide across a table like I've always seen in the movies, and glide straight into a man reloading his semiautomatic. I knock him to the floor, then I grab his gun, turn, and fire. It recoils, and I fall back to the table, but at least I hit him. Dropping it, I turn with my handgun raised, sticking to what I know.

Idris is engaged in hand-to-hand combat with four men. They dart in and out, kicking and punching, but he holds his own. He throws them into tables. One punches at him, but Idris grabs his arm, twists under it, and snaps it before throwing him into the side of the stairs while he screams.

Shit, that's hot.

I notice there are no more, so instead, I head for the stairs, intent on proving my worth. "Bitch," he yells, but he has to concentrate on his fight as I take the steps two at a time, leaping over the broken one I shot.

At the top, I duck and look around.

There are three men in front of a table where I see a scared-looking Bessie hiding. There is a half drank bottle of champagne on her table with empty plates. She's in a skintight, emerald dress and heels, looking pretty as hell. And terrified. Of me.

Of him.

"Hey there, cow!" I call and then duck as a barrage of bullets heads my way. Laughing, I cup my hands around my mouth. "Moo." I wait as they keep firing, and then I hear them stop, knowing they have to be reloading. When I look up, I see them doing just that.

My time to shine, baby. I have to move fast.

Straightening, I aim and fire as I walk. I hit one in the shoulder, and he falls back to the table. I hit the other in the leg, and he crumples with a scream. I miss the third altogether, and my gun clicks empty. Shit. I drop it and try to grab a knife, but he's raising his gun. Suddenly, his head explodes and he falls to the side, and then Idris is there. He looks me over, his eyes narrowed—that tells me I'll be in trouble later.

I can't wait.

He moves to the table, and I skip behind him. Picking up one of their guns, I shoot the other two guards in the chest as Idris takes a seat opposite a scared Bessie. But she sits back, faking confidence, playing the long game as I grab the champagne and sip it while I watch her.

She doesn't even notice me, her eyes trained on him. "Boogeyman," she greets coolly. "To what do I owe the pleasure?"

He simply relaxes in the chair and places his gun on the table as he stares at her. I notice a bead of sweat trickling down her neck and laugh as I chug the bottle.

"I did what I had to," she blurts. "I had a job—"

"You shouldn't have accepted it," is all he says. I finish the bottle and toss it on the floor before perching on one of his legs. He presses his hand to my back to keep me there as they stare at each other.

"Killing me won't change anything. You'll never get to him," she hisses.

"It will sure as shit make me happy," he snaps. "He'll die too, but don't worry, I'm not going to kill you—"

She sits up taller, a flirty smile on her lips. "No? I knew you liked me."

"First, we're going to have some fun," he finishes, and she pales further. He stands and places me on the chair before he rounds the table to tower above her.

"You choose. Your lying mouth or traitorous hands first, Bessie?" he asks, twirling a knife.

"It's Lola," she sneers, and he stabs her hand, pinning it to the table as she screams. Even I wince. Shit, that has to hurt.

"I don't give a fuck. No one will remember your name after today," he growls.

Her other hand slaps the table as she swears and screams at him. Her perfect makeup is ruined as tears slip down her face. She sucks in desperate breaths and her lips quiver, even as she tries to fake her strength. "He'll kill you."

"Nikolić won't—"

She laughs, the sound choked. "Not him. You have no idea who even runs this operation. He owns everything and everyone."

"Even you?" Idris retorts.

She nods. "The bastard probably knew you were coming. That's who I was meeting. He set it up and then left halfway through, wishing me good night. When I said I would see him tomorrow, he just laughed, the fucker. I thought he…"

"He what?" I prompt.

She looks at me, licking her lips, and I see vulnerability there, even through the haze of agony. "Liked me. I was a fool, you will be too. He's untouchable."

"No one is," is all Idris says, having no sympathy for the love-struck girl. She made her choice—a foolish one. One that cost lives and ruined countless others. If he betrayed her, she deserves it.

She deserves everything she gets.

He pulls the knife out, and she falls back with a screech, holding her wounded hand to her chest and ruining her dress as blood coats her skin and the fabric. "You should know criminals have no loyalty to anyone but themselves," Idris snarls.

"Doesn't the same go for assassins?" she counters and looks at me. "He'll kill you, he has to. You know far too much, I'm betting. Don't you know that's what they do? Use people, betray them, and kill them. He told me so."

"The American?" I query.

She nods. "He knows them all somehow, knows Donald."

"That's enough," Idris snaps. "That's not our problem, that's Donald's. You are our problem, one soon to be resolved."

"He'll kill you! Help me get free and I'll—" She tries to convince me, leaning forward in her desperation, but Idris smacks her back. One hit, and she's out cold, her face slack and eyes closed. How boring. He sighs and looks at me.

"She talks too much," I comment, pouting.

"She always did," he replies, "and bakes the worst fucking cookies."

I can't help but laugh and lean forward, running my fingers across the bloody tablecloth. "What shall we do while we wait?" I purr. He smirks, his eyes dropping to my body, but she gasps and wakes up.

Groaning, I sit back. "What a fucking cockblock," I snap as Idris laughs, grabs her half drank glass, and tosses it over her as she sputters.

"Don't pass out just yet, we're about to have fun."

I watch as he teases her, plays with her. If what she says is true, the American sold her out, knew we were coming. Knew we were cleaning house and is allowing us to. Why? But like Idris said, that's not our issue, not our hunt. That's Donald's. We are simply here for revenge, and then…

What? I have no idea. I focus on one second, then the next, the same way I survived.

Her screaming punctures my inner monologue. He cut her dress away, leaving her in her matching panties and bra—she was planning on getting lucky, poor girl—and used it to hang her from the ceiling beam above us. She dangles there, kicking her legs and screaming at him.

Tied up like we were.

He really does have a thoughtful side.

I put my feet up on the white tablecloth and relax as I watch him work. He truly is a master. He knows where to cut, hit, and even burn for maximum pain without making her pass out. It's a beautiful thing to see, like watching an art exhibition… just with more blood.

Like a true sculptor at work.

I tilt my head as I survey her blood dripping down her nearly coated body. He's really fucking angry, and it's fucking hot as hell. His nostrils are flared, and his eyes are hard and narrowed. His fists are clenched, and his muscles are tight. If this is what he does to people who he didn't even trust but annoyed him, then what would he do to someone he truly liked?

I shiver from the thought, my pussy clenching as I imagine all that fury aimed at me. Between her screams, she just cries, resigned but not speaking, giving us nothing. Her loyalty to the American is strong, and my respect for the cow goes up a smidge.

But everyone breaks.

Deciding to move this along so I can get those bloody hands wrapped around my throat while he pounds into me like he's pounding her with his fists, I get up and move to the bar in the corner. There's an ice bucket sitting on the polished black and gold marble bar. I grab it, move behind the bar, and fill it with water in the sink before snatching a slightly dirty towel from the floor. I hesitate before taking a shot of whiskey and knocking it back, the warmth making me shudder. I stride back over to Idris, where he's shaking out his bloody hand.

"Here, try this," I offer.

Idris's head turns, and he looks at the bucket and then at me. "You make me so hard," he growls.

I wink as he takes it, and then I return to my prime position to observe. Pulling her down, he lays her on the table right in front of me, giving me an unobstructed view. Her legs twist as she sobs and fights.

"Please—"

He drapes the cloth over her face and then tips the bucket slowly over it. She chokes as the water fills her mouth, and I smirk, knowing exactly how that feels.

It was one of the first things they did to me. It feels like you're drowning. The water goes up your nose and into your mouth, even when you try to keep it closed. It gets in your eyes so they sting for the next few hours, as does your throat. It's horrible.

Fun to watch though, especially knowing this cunt almost got him killed and ordered me to be tortured. What's that saying? Don't dish out what you can't handle.

Fucking karma, babe.

Her body twists as she struggles, kicking plates off the table. He finally stops pouring and removes the towel as she coughs up water onto her own face. Her eyes are red and her face is soaked as she wheezes and chokes. "Ple—" *Cough.* "Just kill me," she begs breathlessly.

"Just kill you?" he snarls, getting in her face. "Did you just kill me? No, you ordered my torture, you ordered her torture." He jerks his head at me. "You didn't offer mercy, so why should you get it?"

"Please," is all she says as he covers her head again and pours more water. It's sick, but my pussy is wet as hell from watching him hurt her. From watching him make her pay for what she did to us.

He removes it again, and she turns her head, throwing up water as she cries and coughs. Picking up the knife from the table, he presses her other hand down and stabs the blade through her palm, pinning her to the table, and then he does the same with the other before impaling both feet. She passes out during the second stab, but wakes up when he throws the remaining ice-cold water on her face.

She's given up, I see it in her eyes. The retreat, the defeat. How many girls' eyes did she put that look in? How many kids'? Men's? How many families did she destroy? How many mothers sit in their child's empty room, crying, begging, and praying for their children to come home?

How many fathers sit up at night or drink themselves into oblivion to forget their child's face or what might be happening to them right now? She doesn't deserve mercy, she's a monster bigger than either of us. We killed those who deserve it, while she destroyed innocents. Destroyed lives, marriages, and families.

I don't care if this makes us just as bad as her. I remember the innocents' cries, their screams, and hearing them beg for her to kill them. She did that. She deserves every inch of this treatment. Those women could have been lawyers, inventors, counsellors, mothers, and so much more. Their possibilities were endless, their lives had meaning. They had the chance to make an impact on the world in a way only they could. And now they never will. She snatched that away from them, stole their lives like they meant nothing.

She should be as ugly outside as she is inside, showing the rot in her soul.

"You're not worth my time," he eventually snarls an hour later.

I stand, knowing he's had his fun. She's broken, her eyes numb and empty as they roll to him, bloodshot and wounded. "Please, please kill me," she begs again.

"I wonder how many begged you for that," I sneer, even as I pass over his gun. He takes it and shoots, ending her life. It's too easy a death if you ask me.

"We should go," I murmur as we stand side by side, viewing her dead, splayed form. "Won't the police be here… Wait, shouldn't they be here already?"

"Spider stopped them. We have sources on the inside," he explains.

"She deserved more," I reply. "She should have suffered like they did, like I did, known what it was like."

"It's over," is all he says, but I can't walk away. I see that blonde's face in my eyes, the one I'll never know the name of. Whose life I took to save her. I see the countless other scared, empty, angry faces.

I have to do something. Dipping my fingers in her blood, I move to the wall behind her. They have to know. She deserves to be humiliated, embarrassed, exposed, and violated like we were. The unknown masses, the ghosts of her organisation.

She betrayed her fellow women.

I feel Idris watching me as I drag my fingers down the wall, writing a message. It's not eloquent, but they have to know. If any survived, they have to know. I hope they see this. And for those who are part of this, who did this, they should see this too, should see what happens to those who are like her.

They suffer.

I have to re-dip my fingers a few times in her cooling blood, but when it's finished, I step back and stare at the message, feeling slightly better.

*I died screaming, like the countless women I helped traffic.*
*We are coming for you. Evil never wins.*

There.

I grab her phone from her bag, take a picture, and then leak it online. She's in the front, naked and exposed. It's a cruel, horrible thing to do, but I don't give a fuck if it makes me as evil as her. I'm no fucking hero, I'm a goddamn villain. She, *they* made me one.

I'll be a monster to stop people like them so no other woman has to go through what I did, so no more families are ruined.

So the women of this city are safe.

I'll become the very word carved into my stomach.

Bitch.

# CHAPTER TWENTY-SIX

### Idris

She's been quiet since she wrote the message. I clean her hands in the car, and then she stares out of the window as I pull into a parking lot and check over who's left. I shoot a message to Spider as well to make sure the police reports on Lola get leaked and that the images stay up online. It's important to Alena. I can see it. I can see she wants everyone to know.

She wants those who were hurt to know justice was done.
She wants those who did the hurting to know we're coming for them.

She wants it to mean something, for them to pay and suffer like women like her did. My little bitch has a soft heart under all that bloodlust and scars. She wants justice, but instead of trusting those meant to protect her, she's now getting it herself.

Like a true fucking warrior.

"We are going after the guards now, lowlies. We'll kill them and then Nikolić," I vow.

"We finish it," she murmurs and looks over at me. "Make them all pay. I want them all dead so this city is safe once again. We have to."

"We will," I promise as I cup the back of her neck and lean in, pressing my forehead to hers. As I stare into those determined eyes, my heart does a flip, the cold, dead organ beating for her. It's the only time it ever beats faster. It doesn't even increase its rhythm when I'm killing or almost dying.

Only for her.

"I won't kill you, she was wrong," I find myself telling her, searching those golden orbs.

"No?" she whispers.

"No. You're the only thing in this world I fear," I admit, and she blinks in confusion. "I don't fear death. I don't fear pain. I don't even fear everything that comes between that and this. All I fear is you. Letting you close or walking away from you. Alena, Bitch, you reminded me why I do this. For them, for the faceless innocents who suffer in this vile world. I took this job to protect them, to save them, and along the way, that got lost. Tonight, you reminded me why, and now... I fear you. You have the potential to be the only one who gets close to the monster everyone fears. If you betray me, if you die, if you walk away, I'll become the monster they all fear again, maybe even worse."

"That won't happen," she whispers, her eyes filling with tears. "But I'm nobody, just a nobody."

"You're not a nobody to me. You're everything." I swallow, the words are hard. I don't let people close, but she burrowed her way into my black heart during our path of vengeance. Her strength, her mind, her conviction, and ability to walk in the dark with me is slowly becoming everything I didn't know I needed nor wanted. I expected her to be weak, to break, but she surprises me at every turn.

And because of that, she wormed her way into my very fucking soul. The thing I didn't think I had anymore. What happens when this is over? I don't know, but I fear her because…

Fuck, because I care.

We stare at each other, neither of us knowing what to say or do until my phone vibrates, alerting me to police approaching the restaurant. We both turn and watch them pull up with their sirens blaring.

"I fear you too," she confesses without looking at me. "I fear how important you have become to me. I don't want to depend on anyone.

Down in that hell hole, I found myself, found that I need no one." She looks at me. "But I want you."

What else is there to say?

We both know this thing we have going has a time limit. It cannot last. An assassin can't... love. Trust. Have a weakness. And she needs to heal and find a place to feel safe again.

I can't be that.

Or can I?

---

WE DON'T SPEAK MUCH AFTER THAT, INSTEAD REFOCUSING ON OUR mission. The streets of the city run red with the deaths we execute together. We move quickly through the list as night seeps in, the streets busy as the city comes alive, but tonight, it's filled with hesitation. Even strangers on the streets feel the anticipation of violence in the air.

The next one we hit leads us to the stables on the edge of the park. The horses are all in their stalls, apart from four that are tethered up and ready to be taken out. There are a few workers milling around, but I flash my gun and jerk my head, clearing them out. They get the hint and run, leaving us alone with the man we are here for.

He's in a stall at the back, wearing a shirt and tight jeans with AirPods in his ears. He's clearly here to ride his horse or check on it. Idiot doesn't even hear us coming, too busy jamming out to... yep, Vengaboys.

Fucking hell, this one needs to be fast.

I open the stall, and the horse huffs at me and turns. It alerts the man, and as he spins around, I go to grab him, but Alena is there. She takes a rake and knocks him the fuck out with it. I turn to her, blinking as she shrugs innocently. He's passed out on the floor, nose bleeding. Reaching down, I grab his legs and drag him from the stall as Alena coos at the horse.

"Pretty boy," she purrs and shuts the door. "Sorry about this. Your daddy is a cunt, you'll be better without him," she assures him and blows a kiss before following me. I throw him into the back wall near the hay and tack, and then crouch down before him, waiting for him to come around. He's groaning, pale, and weak, so it shouldn't be long.

Alena sits on the hay at the side, swinging her legs back and forth. As soon as he wakes up, he starts shrieking. Lovely. I can't even get any sense out of him, the fucking pussy, so I give up trying. I stand and leave him to scream, grabbing some of the ropes from the wall and wrapping them around my knuckles. I tug, testing them.

"Shit, okay, you're using ropes on me later," Alena purrs, and I wink over at her before moving to the horses. They toss their heads nervously, but I stroke their noses, talking softly to them until they settle. Animals have always liked me, it's my only fucking saving grace.

Moving slowly so I don't scare them, I tie one rope onto each of the four horses before reaching down and grabbing the screaming man's arms and legs. It's a difficult manoeuvre, but I manage to tie him to all four. I untie the horses and urge them on. Two to the back, two to the front. They move slowly at first as he screams louder, so I tap their asses until they buck and rush off.

Tearing his limbs from his body.

They stop at the door though and turn around, so I quickly untie the ropes and put them in the stalls—I'm a monster, not evil. I leave the dismembered body for someone else to clean up as Alena skips by my side as we leave.

"That was cool as shit," she remarks. "Real Henry the VIII shit."

I snort but carry on walking as we head to our next victim.

One is tossed from a building, another is tied to a cement brick and pitched into the river to drown. Alena guts one and bleeds out another hung from a streetlight before we hit the last name on the list.

It's harder to find him, I have to hack into some systems. I'm not as good as Spider, but I manage, and it eventually leads us to Happy Endings—a massage parlour with a twist. It's staffed by stolen girls and foreign women who are forced to earn their way out. They have more freedom than the trafficked girls, but not by much.

We go through the backdoor, and the security is easy to get through. Soothing spa music plays, and we pass the girls' shower and changing room. Their living quarters are most likely in the basement—it's not the first place like this I've raided.

We pass those rooms, ignoring the girls who look at us. They know better than to question two free people in this place. I bet it looks like Alena is a new girl or mine. I don't do anything to make them believe otherwise, needing to blend in.

Stepping through another door, we reach the front area of the massage place where the actual client rooms are, and the doors shut behind us with a lock, proving they can only come out when called. It's much nicer up front. There are stone walls with hanging candles, and it exudes money and relaxation. A woman comes from a room, tying her robe. She has tears in her eyes, her hair is a mess, and her body is bare beneath her covering. She looks up and freezes, then rushes past us, her head lowered.

Alena snarls, pulls her knife, and storms to the room. I should drag her back and focus on what we're here for, but I don't. She busts in the door, slamming it behind her, but I follow. The man is buttoning his slacks. He looks like a banker type, all rich businessman and slicked hair. His gold wedding band gleams on his hand.

"Another girl?" he questions, then sees me and frowns. "What the —I didn't rough her up, I know that's extra. What's going on?"

I kick the door shut behind me and cross my arms so he can't leave while Alena prowls towards him. "Did she consent?" she snarls.

"What?"

She gets right in his face and pushes him back to the rumpled massage bed.

"Did she fucking consent? You know the word 'yes'? What about 'silent'? Did she stay silent? Did she want to say no but was too scared to? Or did you not even bother to ask, you sick fucking rapist?" she almost yells. It's a good thing these rooms aren't monitored and they're soundproof. It's members only, after all. You have to pay, and if you kill a girl... well, in their mind, there are plenty of them on the streets.

In fact, if you pay high enough, you can do whatever the fuck you want to them.

He doesn't respond, and she presses the knife to his mouth. "What, nothing to say? Does that mean you consent to me cutting your pretty boy face up?"

He goes to speak, and she presses the blade's tip to the edge of his lips and slashes sideways. He howls, falling back as his cheek and lip flop open. She quickly does the other side before ripping his shirt open. Buttons fly everywhere as he hits the bed, his hands clutching his face as blood pours from the wounds.

While wielding the knife, she looks up at him. "I'm going to give you a message you will never forget." With that, she gets to work, and when she steps back, he passes out. I raise my eyebrows.

She carved 'I'm a rapist pig' down his stomach.

"Why not kill him?" I ask.

"Because now he'll suffer more. He'll have to live with that on his chest and see it all his life. His wife will know, his family, his job. He'll be ruined. He'll hit rock bottom, and he'll probably die," she reasons as she turns. "It will destroy him more."

Fuck, that's evil and so goddamn incredible.

I crook my finger at her, and she walks up to me. When she reaches me, I grab her hair and yank her head back, kissing her hard before pulling away. "Good."

We leave him there. Either he'll die or wake up and have to go home. She's right—he'll suffer more. We check the other rooms, finding them empty until we reach the last one where our target currently is. His pale chubby ass jiggles as he thrusts, fucking the woman bent over the bed. She's silently crying, her hands digging into the bed. His belt is wrapped around her neck to control her like a fucking sex toy or animal as he grunts and sweats.

Without hesitation, I shoot him in the leg. He screeches and jerks from the force before falling on the woman. She cries out, shoving at him, and I pull him away from her gently. I can't help but see the blood smeared across her ass and pussy. He ripped her. She cries and scurries to the wall, sliding down it with her arms wrapped around her stomach.

Alena goes to her, holding her hands out as she crouches before the sobbing woman. "We won't hurt you. We are here to help. Can you walk?"

The woman nods, swallowing hard as I restrain the screaming man.

"Good, go and get the others and wait there. We'll come back. I promise."

With one last look at me, the woman rushes to her feet and then leaves the room. Alena turns and glares at the bleeding man. "Make it hurt," she demands before leaning back against the wall, her eyes narrowed in fury.

So I do. Grabbing the hot stones on the side, I force one into his mouth and one into his ass, and then I pour the hot wax across his cock while she observes. We watch it sizzle as he chokes and tries to scream. I wait until he passes out, and then I kill him.

I tear his throat out and leave him there with the stone in his ass, his tiny burnt cock hanging out. We head towards the women, finding the one we saved in the dressing room with three others who look scared.

"Where are the others?" I ask.

"Downstairs." They point at a tiny staircase in the back corner, and I nod.

"Management?"

They swallow and point out of the room. "Out front, past the rooms."

"Stay here," I tell Alena, and for once, she listens as I move back down the hallway, following it around to a set of double doors. Through it is a waiting room with three men reading newspapers or scrolling on their phones. I shoot the ceiling.

"Out, unless you want to die, you sick bastards. If I see you again, you're dead," I threaten, and then turn to a man grabbing a shotgun from behind the desk. Firing, I knock him back to his swivel seat and then move past him to the manager's office where the door is opening. A heavyset, balding man covered in way too much gold jewellery stands in the doorframe.

I shoot him too, not bothering with small talk. He won't know enough to help me. In his office, I find a safe, which I open with his fingerprint and eye. There are thousands inside. I pack it into two bags, grab his keys, and return to Alena where she helped the girls get dressed.

"Here." I toss one of the bags at their feet. "Share this between you." Keeping hold of the other bag, I head downstairs. The door at the bottom is made of metal with a sliding hatch. Unlocking and opening it, I step in and recoil at the living conditions.

Alena steps up to my side and gasps. "Fuckers," she snarls.

They live side by side in cots with barely any blankets and zero privacy. They're all sleeping in cheap lingerie, their makeup and hair ready so they don't get hurt. There's a toilet and a sink in the corner, nothing else. There are even bars on the windows. It's disgusting, and they all look scared until Alena explains the situation. We leave them to make their escape, giving them the money we found upstairs. I know Donald will send in clean-up and get all the client lists to hunt them down. He may even use some of it as leverage—who knows? But that's their job. We are nearing the end of ours.

All the guards, partners, enticers, and runners are dead. That only leaves one man.

It's Nikolić's turn.

# CHAPTER TWENTY-SEVEN

### Alena

It's early morning now. We have been hunting and killing all day and most of the night. I'm tired, but not willing to give up. We are ending this before sunrise. Idris knows where to go, and when we get there, he adds more weapons to his frame and passes me several.

"He'll have protection," is all he says. We are outside a mansion on the outskirts of the city. One of those godawful, old money ones. The iron gate is shut up tight with the lights peeking through the windows, alerting us they are home.

He's right. I see men patrolling the grounds as we wait parked in the trees opposite the property. "Stay here for a minute," he murmurs, then leaves me sitting in the dark. I watch him crouch and run across the road before the mansion, but then he blends into the night.

Like a ghost.

He comes back a moment later and has something in his hand. He winks at me and mouths, "Boom," and then a massive explosion rocks the complex, blowing the gates open and throwing three men into the air. I watch the fire and smoke as he guns the SUV forward. He rams through what's left of the twisted metal, drives over the men and debris, and pulls right up to the giant, white double doors under the columned arch. Men stream from the door, brought by the noise, and shoot at our car. I duck when it sounds like hail is hitting the vehicle, but they don't pierce it, thank fuck.

I dart my gaze up when I hear Idris moving. He pulls the pin on something, tosses it out of the window, and then covers me as we press into the seat. Another explosion rocks the earth, and rubble hits the car this time. He's moving in a second, getting out of the SUV and firing into the smoking mass as my ears ring from the noise.

I watch him clear the doorway and then gesture for me to follow. Gripping my gun tighter, I slip from the smoking car and race up the steps. When I'm behind him, he moves into the room, low and fast, sweeping the space with his gun as he checks it. The entrance is a huge lobby, with a massive chandelier hanging down above us. It has white tile floors, and to the left is a curved staircase with a black banister where a man is currently descending. Idris shoots him. To the right are two doors, which frame an oil painting above a table with flowers. Beyond that is a hallway that leads to the back of the house and who knows what.

They clearly have more money than sense, blood money, earned from flesh trading, the fucker. It makes me want to ruin it all, though Idris has already made a good dent in that with the gate and car and bodies littered about.

"He'll be upstairs. Go first, I'll watch our backs," he orders. I nod, feeling shocked he trusts me to go first. Holding the gun securely, I ascend the first steps sideways, my heart hammering. Adrenaline surges through my veins. I glance over to see him walking backwards, scanning everything, his gun ready.

He's trusting me, and that's huge, but I have to focus on our job. One wrong move, and not only do I get myself killed, but him too. I'm okay with dying for revenge, but not him.

Not anyone else for my cause.

The railing runs across a balcony at the top, which overlooks the landing with hallways to the left and right. I press against the wall near the top and look left and see no one, so I move to the other side to look right and have to fall backwards as a shot hits the corner where I just was. Idris catches me, slamming me to the wall as we wait the person out.

When they stop firing, Idris pulls another grenade and tosses it down the corridor. A few seconds later, it detonates, and he rushes up the stairs, races around the corner, and fires. I glance back to make sure no one is sneaking up on us before following after him.

There are two dead men, one in pieces and one with a gunshot wound leaning against the wall, which is coated in gore. Idris checks rooms as he passes, and I rush after him as he clears another. He waits for me at the next door, his hand on the doorknob as I stop before it, gun at the ready. I nod, and he rips it open. I go in firing, hitting the man sleeping in the bed with noise cancelling headphones on. I make sure no one else is in there, and then I leave. We have to clear five more rooms before we reach a study at the end.

The door's locked. This has to be it. I can't believe it. He thought it would keep us out, but I'm betting it's simply to buy time while more of his men and guards arrive. Or it's just a last stand. Who knows?

The gold doorknob gleams above the lock, and I lean down to try and peek through it. I only catch a glimpse of sofas and a TV. Standing upright, I look to Idris for what to do. I thought he would pick it or check it, but he simply rams his body into it, breaking the door open as he rolls inside. I stay out when a gun goes off, not wanting to be hit as he manages to move behind the sunken brown sofa. There's a gold framed TV on the wall behind it, and two big bay windows on either side. The carpeted floor is covered in shards of wood from the door, and on the back wall are huge monitors featuring CCTV camera feeds. Not just of the house, but also the city, and I'm betting places where they keep women.

That means the shooter, Nikolić, has to be to the right. I quickly pass the broken doorway and press against the other side of the door to try and see.

He's crouching behind a huge white desk, his computer and papers on the floor. His arms are braced on the surface, and his gun is aimed right at Idris's head, which is poking above the sofa, his size hindering him. He smirks, knowing he's got him. He's going to fire.

Going to shoot Idris dead.

Not while I'm fucking here.

Taking aim, I ground myself. I have one shot, otherwise he'll turn that gun on me. Knowing I'm in the open, knowing I have no protection, I do it anyway. He dies, I die. I squeeze the trigger, my heart skipping a beat as time seems to slow down.

I watch it sail through the air, and then suddenly, time speeds back up as it hits him right in the shoulder, throwing him backwards as Idris looks over at me in shock, his mouth open wide. My hands tremble slightly as I drop the gun. I meet Idris's eyes again. He knows.

I see the truth in his gaze. He knows I just nearly got myself killed to protect him. With his eyes, he warns me that's not the end of it before he stands and rushes around the desk, dragging Nikolić up and throwing him over it. Nikolić lands on the carpet with a groan, and I step into the room, watching as Idris rounds it again to stand above him, gun aimed at his head.

"You'll die like your brother did, begging for your meagre fucking life."

Footsteps sound behind me, and I turn in time to see at least twenty men rushing up the stairs and into the hallway. Fuck. I grab a side table, throw it in front of the damaged door, and duck as they start firing. Gripping my gun tighter, I wait until there's a break, and then I fire back before ducking and glancing at Idris. His face is in a snarl, and he's lost in a haze of bloodlust as he pummels his fist into Nikolić. He doesn't even seem to hear the gun fight going on.

*Shit.*

"Idris!" I yell as I duck lower, holding my hands over my head as I wait out the shots.

He looks at me, his fist held in the air, Nikolić's shirt clutched in his other hand. "Keep firing!" he shouts and turns back, punching him again as Nikolić hangs limply from his grasp.

*Fuck!*

I fire back blindly as the walls explode next to me, plaster and wood raining down. I can barely hear over the gunshots, barely see or think. Still, I keep shooting, giving him his chance for revenge like he gave me, even though it's probably going to get me killed. I jump when a bullet whizzes past my ear, that was too close. Sitting up, I fire with a scream as my blood drips down my ear. I hit two, but it's not enough.

"Idris!" I scream desperately, needing him. I look back as my gun clicks empty. He snarls, releasing Nikolić and turning to me. He's choosing me rather than his revenge. He slides across the floor to my side, swinging his weapon up as I grab the spare from his waistband. Together we hold the surge at bay, pushing them back. We kill them, even though it means Nikolić has time to start crawling away.

When the last guard is down, we look around, panting and covered in debris and blood. Where is that Serbian bastard?

Then I see him. He's climbing out of a window. Fuck. I drop my gun and run. Idris deserves his revenge. I throw myself at him, grabbing his shirt as he leaps. I fall to the floor, yanking him back in and on top of me. He elbows me, and I grunt, but I wrap myself around him as his elbow connects with my face again. I keep him there until Idris reaches us after checking the hall. He grabs Nikolić, dragging him into the air as I roll onto my back, my nose dripping blood.

Idris meets my eyes, sees the blood, and goes wild.

He slaps him around like a rag doll, throwing him into the walls and around the room as I sit up and watch. Eventually, he gets tired when Nikolić stops fighting, and Idris tosses him to the ground near me. "If you weren't already a dead man before, now you are. No one hurts my bitch," he snarls, pulling out his knife and stabbing it through the side of his head.

No drama, no movie lines.

He kills him, ending his reign of terror.

With a grunt, he pulls it free before looking at me. "Let's go." I nod, and he helps me to my feet. On our way out of the room, he freezes and meets my eyes. "Go, I'll meet you outside." I frown but do as I'm told, walking past the corpses and chaos to the front of the house, where I wait anxiously at the door. I hear him moving around, and then about two minutes later, he comes down the stairs with a smirk.

"I set a fire," is all he says, and I laugh. We step outside into the early morning light, the sun rising and fresh. Clean. It's a new day, it's a new me.

I feel... sad almost. My revenge is over. They are dead. I achieved everything I wanted. I turn to watch flames lick at the windows of the house and crawl through the building.

So... what do I do now? I feel useless.

Idris comes to my side as we watch the house burn, both of us silent. The quiet after a storm.

We stand in the destruction of the smoking, flaming house. Bullets and guns are everywhere, and bodies litter the floor. Blood covers the once pristine walls, and our car is still perched on the front portico.

"What now?" I ask as I sit on the step next to the car and watch the sun rise over the horizon. "I can't go back to my old life. Yet there is no place for me." I look up at him then, but he crouches next to me, watching the sunrise. I turn back. He's silent.

I'm silent as well. He's going to leave me here, he has to, doesn't he?

His phone rings, and he answers, putting it on speaker. "I take it it's done? I have calls from police and fire departments, and a whole lot of alarms going off." Donald sighs.

"It's done."

"Good, so what now, Boogeyman? Can I expect you to die again, or are you back for good?"

He looks at me then, his dark eyes running across my face. "I'm back, but I have a new partner." He hangs up.

"Partner?" I repeat.

Leaning closer, he cups my bloody, aching cheek. "You were right. I was running, hiding from what I am, but no more. If you want, we can be partners. We'll find a new life together. A new balance."

"Really?" I query, searching his face. "What happened to wanting peace? To retirement?"

"I'd rather have you," he replies, making my heart flip as emotion overwhelms me. For so long, I've been alone, scared, and angry. Now I have a new life, a new dawn, and my heart isn't as dark as it once was.

I throw myself at him, sealing my lips to his as he chuckles, his hand cuffing my neck. "Is that a yes?"

"Yes," I murmur against his lips.

Yes, I'll be your partner.

Yes, I'll be yours.

Just… hell fucking yes.

## CHAPTER TWENTY-EIGHT

### Idris

I steal one of Nikolić's sports cars from the garage around back. Alena drives, her hair blowing in the wind as she grins and screams, gunning it down the roads as the sun fills the sky. I can't help but stare at her, she takes my breath away. She glances over at me with a full grin before facing the road.

I made the right choice. I couldn't watch her walk away. I just couldn't. She's got a talent for this life, but more than that, she has awakened something within me, something I thought long dead—humanity, feelings. My soul is vibrant and my heart beats again for Alena, only for Alena.

I give her directions, and we pull into the garage before riding the elevator up. Spider and Donald are waiting for us.

"It's done," I tell them.

They look us over, and Donald smiles. "I knew it would be."

"The American?" I inquire.

"Don't worry about that," Donald replies and shares a look with Spider. "We have it covered."

I nod and turn, and Donald calls out, "So you're fully back… and Alena is staying?"

I nod, and he grins at me, even as Spider laughs. "Is Boogeyman finding his heart? Maybe even falling in love?" he jokes, and I pull my gun out to shoot him, but Alena stops me with a hand on my shoulder, so I begrudgingly put it away.

"I take my own jobs," I grit out. "I choose them this time."

"Very well. You are fully reinstated. As for Alena, she will need training," Donald murmurs. I jerk, stepping before her. She will not be going through the training we did. All four of us, Donald, Max, Spider, and myself. It wasn't training, it was hell, it was war.

"No," I snarl, and he narrows his eyes in warning.

"She will need to be trained if I'm to trust her—"

"I will train her," I snarl.

They both go silent, knowing I've never offered that before, even the many times they have ordered it. "Very well. For now, go and get some rest and a shower. You both need it," he teases, his nose crinkled.

"Oh, Alena?" Spider calls. "I cleaned your trail. I thought you should know you're dead."

"What?" she asks, confused.

"I'm sorry. You were missing for so long, it seems they declared you dead and buried you. There's an empty grave at Cherry Cemetery on the hill."

"Well shit, I guess I'm a ghost too," she jokes, and I grin at her. "Thanks."

"Don't forget you have a family here now, and when you're ready, my girl would love to meet you. You would get on really well, she's like us. Welcome to the family," Spider offers, saluting her.

"To the Clergy," Donald toasts.

I know this isn't a formal welcome, she will need testing and tatting, but for now, it will do. She has their blessing, their protection. Above that, she has mine. No one will ever hurt her again, or they will die by my hand.

We leave in the same car, with me driving this time, but once I get on the road, I don't know where to go. Where is home?

The city, like when I was an assassin?

Or the country, like when I was a dead man?

"Where to, big guy?" She grins and lays her hand on my thigh. "Preferably somewhere with a shower and a bed." She winks.

I look at her as I pull up at a red light. She's right. Wherever she is, that's where I'll be. Home isn't just a place, it's a feeling. It's wherever you feel safe, comfortable, and happy.

She's that for me.

She's home.

# CHAPTER TWENTY-NINE

### Idris
*Three months later...*

The summer breeze blows through the open front door as I paint the living room wall a deep, navy blue. My heart is slow and peaceful, my mind not on alert. I'm home, I came back... we came back here. It seemed like the right thing to do. We are close enough to the city to work, and far enough away to have the space and peace we both need to heal, to live.

She slotted right into my life like she has always been here, and we've been renovating ever since we got back. It turns out I have horrible taste, so she's in charge, I'm just the muscle. The thought makes me smile as I hear her swearing at the flowers outside. She may be an excellent killer, a fucking brilliant lover, and better partner, but she doesn't possess a green thumb. In fact, I caught her ranting at the plants last night, threatening them, when she couldn't sleep. Even remembering it has my heart warming. She's the only person who could ever have done that.

She was an unexpected complication. For assassins like me, she was a wrench thrown into the works. A bad move, a mistake. I know better now. She's everything I have been looking for. I left in search of something, something I was unaware of.

It was her.

I thought I needed peace, needed the small-town life to save what was left of myself, but I was wrong. She showed me that I didn't need to change who I am to be happy. To find peace with myself, I needed to be me, Boogeyman, a killer... to find her.

The woman who stole my heart and soul in a dungeon. Who walked through fire with me, who killed for me, with me. All this time, I thought I left to search for a place. Instead, I left to find her.

A person.

My person.

My bitch.

She sighs as she comes in, and I can't help but run my eyes down her body. She's been gardening all morning and is coated in a thin layer of sweat, making her now tanned skin glisten. She's put on weight as well, and her hips and ass are my new favourite things, especially in the tiny blue shorts she's wearing, her thick thighs rubbing together as she walks. Her feet are bare, and her hair is tied back in a red bandana. Her tits are encased in a see-through crop top, which is driving me wild, and the scar on her stomach is fully healed now, the white jagged marks proudly announcing, "Bitch."

Fuck, she makes me so hard. How can one person be so perfect? She notices me staring and grins. "Want to do another kind of work out, big guy?" she purrs. I drop the brush and advance on her, hunting her with a grin as she laughs before backing up and turning. "Gotta catch me first, assassin!"

With that, she turns and races away, not fake running to be caught. No, she fucking sprints, leaping over boxes and furniture. Snarling, I burst into action, chasing her. She makes it out of the backdoor, doing a leap roll, and is on her feet in an instant, but I'm too fast.

She can never escape me. She's my eternal prey.

I grab her and haul her over my shoulder and back into the house, kicking the door shut as I slam her into the wall, rip her shorts open, and shove my hand inside to cup her wet pussy. She groans, wrapping her legs around my waist as her hands grip my face and her lips smash into mine. She bites and licks, giving as good as she gets.

Just like she did from the start. Just a voice through a wall. Now I can't live without her. Not that I was living before her. No, I was surviving, waiting for her to explode into my life. Tearing my mouth away, I rest my forehead against hers, breathing heavily as I look into those golden eyes. They were once filled with such anger, but now they are filled with love, happiness, and determination.

Purpose.

She might think I helped save her, but in reality, she saved me.

She brought me back from the brink, she gave me a life.

She gave a killer a heart.

"Fuck me," she demands, and I do as I'm told, having her screaming in no time.

---

## Alena

THE GRAVE PROTRUDES FROM THE GROUND BEFORE ME. THERE ARE NO flowers, no well wishes, or other signs anyone has been here. As if the grave is forgotten, as if she never existed. No one remembered her, no one cared.

*Alena Shaw.*

That's it, my name with the date. I stand before it, feeling almost sad. I worked so hard in my life, and I thought I lived it to its fullest, but I guess you never really know who will be there when it gets hard or who will remember you.

At least I still have a chance to make a difference. That Alena is dead, and in her place is a stronger, more confident, happier—and yes, more scarred—warrior version. And with my assassin at my side, I can do anything. I can make this world mine, and I know I'll never be alone again.

He'll remember me, he'll care.

He'll never leave me, I see it in his eyes every time he looks at me, all the words he can't say. He struggles with emotions and is still learning how to love. I guess I am too. I still wake up with nightmares, but my Boogeyman is there to scare them away. Sometimes I flinch or get angry when I think about what happened.

He's taught me how to channel it, use it. He's been training me every day for the last three months. Sometimes I want to kill him when I'm exhausted and covered in sweat. He puts me through night drills, weapons training, hand-to-hand combat, survival training, all of it. I feel like I joined the military, but I actually think this may be harder. He doesn't go easy on me because we're sleeping together, because we live together. No, he's tougher on me than anyone else. Spider came to check up on us and watched a drill, and he actually felt sorry for me. He even brought his partner, Nadia. He was right—we get on well. It's nice to know there is a family of people out there like us.

As for Idris... well, he makes up for it by making me come all night. In the spare moments we have, we decorate our house, fashioning it how we both always imagined.

Our refuge from the world.

"Nobody missed her," I comment as I look up at him, the man who is always by my side. The monster they avoid in the streets, the killer even killers run from. Yet here he stands with his hand in mine, offering comfort when I need it.

He looks down at me and frowns. "Then they are fools."

"Would you miss me?" I tease.

He turns me, presses me to the stone, and grips my throat hard. "I won't ever need to miss you, you'll be right here for the rest of our lives, Bitch," he snarls.

"Promise, Boogeyman?" I whisper.

"Promise," he rumbles, and then he leans down and kisses me as his phone rings. He pulls it out and answers, his eyes still on mine. He's only inches away, so I hear everything.

"I have a job for you both, one mil contract. Target is a Russian general, so pack your passports. There's a jet waiting at the strip. Do you accept?" I hear Donald ask.

He arches his eyebrow, and I smirk. "Hell yes."

"You heard her," he says and hangs up, leaning down to kiss me. "I love you." It's so quiet that I blink as I pull back.

"You better. I didn't save your ass from that dungeon just for your gun." I grin, and he rolls his eyes.

"Shut the fuck up before I make you. We need to prepare." He pulls me away without letting me glance back at the gravestone. It's my past, after all, and the man at my side is my future, and the future looks fucking bright.

Bloody, but bright.

As we walk from the cemetery, I hear gunshots in the distance echoing through the city.

This city is going to war, and although it's not our fight, our story is far from over. Down in that dungeon, I found my purpose, my place in this world. It's not what I thought it would be, but with my assassin at my side, I know I can survive anything.

Together.

It may have started with revenge, but it ends with love and plenty of fucking death.

After all, I'm an assassin now.

Boogeyman's bitch.

ENJOYED THE STORY?

*Read the two other books set in this same world now!*
Scarlett Limerence & Nadia's Salvation

# ABOUT K.A KNIGHT

K.A Knight is an indie author trying to get all of the stories and characters out of her head. She loves reading and devours every book she can get her hands on, she also has a worrying caffeine addiction.

She leads her double life in a sleepy English town, where she spends her days writing like a crazy person.

**Read more at K.A Knight's website
or join her Facebook Reader Group.**

**Sign up for exclusive content and my newsletter here**

facebook.com/KatieKnightAuthor
twitter.com/K_AKnight
instagram.com/katieknightauthor
amazon.com/K-A-Knight/e/B07H4GKJBC
goodreads.com/K_A_Knight

# ALSO BY K.A KNIGHT

**THEIR CHAMPION SERIES**

The Wasteland

The Summit

The Cities

The Nations

Their Champion Coloring Book

The Forgotten

The Lost

The Damned

**DAWNBREAKER SERIES**

Voyage to Ayama

Dreaming of Ayama

**THE LOST COVEN SERIES**

Aurora's Coven

Aurora's Betrayal

**HER MONSTERS SERIES**

Rage

Hate

**THE FALLEN GODS SERIES**

Pretty Painful

Pretty Bloody

Pretty Stormy

Pretty Wild

Pretty Hot

Pretty Faces

Pretty Spelled

### STAND-ALONES

Scarlett Limerence

Nadia's Salvation

The Standby

Den of Vipers

Daddy's Angel

Diver's Heart

### AUDIOBOOKS

Den of Vipers

The Wasteland

The Summit

Rage

Hate

---

### HER FREAKS SERIES
**Co-Written with Erin O'Kane**

Circus Save Me

Taming The Ringmaster

### THE WILD BOYS SERIES
**Co-Written with Erin O'Kane**

The Wild Interview

The Wild Tour

The Wild Finale

The Wild Boys Boxed Set

### THE FORSAKEN
**Co-Written with Loxley Savage**

Capturing Carmen

Stealing Shiloh

Harboring Harlow

---

### CO-WRITTEN STAND-ALONES
**Co-Written with Erin O'Kane**

The Hero Complex

Dark Temptations (contains One Night Only and Circus Saves Christmas)

**Co-Written with Kendra Moreno & Poppy Woods**

Shipwreck Souls

The Horror Emporium

**Co-Written with Loxley Savage**

Gangsters & Guns

Printed in Great Britain
by Amazon